D1478296

# Home to Beulah

*A genealogy mystery*

## Claudia C. Breland

Cover photo:
The cottage on Crystal Lake, circa 1965
From the personal collection of the author

ISBN-13: 978-0-9600793-1-5

For Summer Catherine
That you may know the beauty
of Northern Michigan

# Other books by this author

Genealogy Offline: A Guide to Family History
Records That are not Online

Searching for Your Ancestors in Historic
Newspapers

At Home in Lansing: The Journals of
Maurice L. Reed, 1927-1931

Lansing and Beyond: The Journals of
Maurice L. Reed, 1932-1934

On the Banks of the Pee Dee:
The Ancestry of Mary Gladys Jordan Sells

From Pie Stand to Icon:
The 100 Year History of The Cherry Hut
Beulah, Michigan

At age 22, Grace Dorsch has her hands full keeping house for her father, stepmother and two younger siblings in 1920s Detroit, Michigan. Suddenly, a letter announcing a bequest of a cottage in the tiny village of Beulah, in northern Michigan, turns her world upside down. Awaiting her there are new friends and further puzzles to solve: who willed the cottage to Grace, and who is resorting to violence to force her out of it? Was she born in Detroit or in Beulah, and was Herman Dorsch really her father? A genealogy mystery with timeless implications and old-fashioned, on-the-ground research, this will be enjoyed by genealogists and non-genealogists alike!

# Michigan's Lower Peninsula

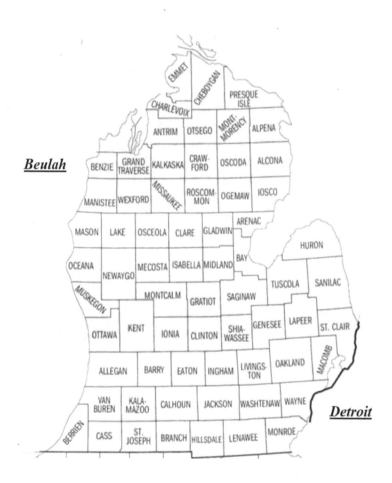

Adapted from the county map at Michigan GenWeb:
https://www.migenweb.org/map.htm

*Standard Atlas of Benzie County, Michigan* (Chicago: Geo. Ogle & Co., 1915), 7, PDF download, *Internet Archive* (http://www.archive.org)

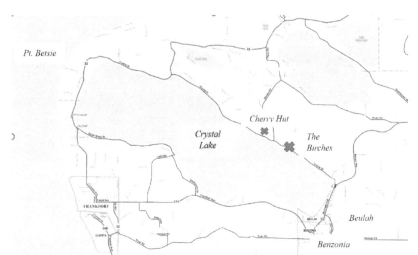

Adapted from an online map of Benzie County, Michigan: https://www.mapofus.org/_maps/dot/mi/Benzie.pdf

# Contents

# Prologue

Beulah, Michigan
April 1902

The young woman was dressed in black from head to foot, even though it had been over a year since her husband died. Looking for the tenth time down the railroad tracks, she paced the wooden deck of the Beulah train depot, another woman holding a nine-month-old baby on a bench nearby. "Lottie," the woman with the baby urged, "here, take your daughter for a moment. I have something I want to give you."

Lottie Warren turned and smiled at the one bright spot in her life, her daughter Grace. "Come to mama, love," she said softly. "Edith, you don't need to give me anything; you've done so much for me already!"

"I still don't understand why you need to go off into the wilds of Detroit to find your way in life. I should think you'd be able to find it right here in Benzie County." Edith knew it was no use in trying to dissuade Lottie from this new religion her friend had found. Edith had read many newspaper articles on "Eddyism" as the Germans called it and was familiar with the fervent beliefs of new converts. She was also becoming too familiar with the stories of those who died because of it and was dreading Lottie's possible fate.

"Then consider this a gift for Grace; when she's old enough you can buy her some good books." Edith Van Wagoner smiled at her friend. "Remember those good times we had at the Academy?"

Lottie laughed. "And just think, now you're teaching at the one-room schoolhouse in Thompsonville!" She teased, "And I just bet you've set your sights higher — like teaching at college somewhere!" Lottie sobered. "With Edward gone, and Father dead, I just need to strike out on my own. Surely you can understand that?"

Edith sighed and tucked the envelope in Lottie's reticule. She gave Lottie one last hug as the train pulled in. "Be sure to write — I'll haunt the mailbox until you do!" Watching as Lottie and baby Grace boarded the train, she fought back tears. Somehow, deep in her heart, she knew she would never see them again.

# Chapter 1: Life in Detroit

Detroit, Michigan
April 1923

With a feeling of satisfaction, Grace Dorsch hung the last shirt on the line and bent to pick up the empty clothes basket. Heading to the back porch and making her way through the clutter of wash tub and wringer, stacks of firewood and two old bicycle tires, she saw her best friend Chloe McGrath coming around the corner of the house, waving a couple of tickets in the air. The sunlight glinted off her red-gold hair as she trotted up the porch steps behind Grace.

"Hey, look what I've got! Tickets to the lecture at the new branch library!" In a dramatic voice, reading from the slip of cardboard in her hand, she proclaimed, "Hear an interesting paper entitled 'Memories of Old Detroit' given by Mr. Clarence M. Burton on Wednesday next...."[1]

Grace interrupted her before she could finish. Turning to open the screen door, she sighed. "You know I can't go to that. I've got too much work to do. Besides, I don't want

---

[1] Clarence M. Burton (1853-1932) was a Detroit lawyer and philanthropist. The Burton Collection of local history at the Detroit Public Library is named for him.

to listen to Papa sniffing about 'people who think they're better than we are'. I'm lucky if I can go to the library once a month. Not that I have much time to read," she concluded.

As the two girls made their way into the kitchen, Chloe changed the subject. Lowering her voice, she asked, "Have you found out anything more about your mother?"

"You mean other than that she died when I was a baby? No. Papa doesn't like to talk about her, and besides, he says that what is past is past, and I've got a perfectly good stepmother now." She glanced at the clock. "The pie should be ready to take out of the oven; time to start on the biscuits." Continuing the conversation, Grace said, "Papa has always been so silent — it's hard to know what he's thinking. But Mama and the twins sure make up for it!"

With a practiced hand, she opened the oven door, and with a couple of thick dish towels, removed a fragrant peach pie and set it on the drainboard to cool. Closing the oven door, she wiped her forehead and ran a hand through her short blonde curls. "You'd think now that I'm almost twenty-two, I wouldn't cause such an uproar by cutting my hair! The way Papa reacted you would have thought I'd painted my face!" Chloe laughed and agreed. "My folks were a little less shocked, but not by much. Short hair sure is easier to take care of, though."

Grace closed the oven door and turned to the icebox for the ingredients for the biscuits: butter and buttermilk, and to the free-standing pantry for the flour and baking powder. Grace had made these so many times she no longer needed to refer to the recipe, the same as she'd memorized all her other favorites: cottage cheese dumplings, veal croquettes, and her masterpiece, devil's food cake.

Chloe and Grace continued chatting about their day — Chloe about her job as a waitress and Grace about the stolen looks she'd gotten at today's *Detroit Free*

*Press.* "Did you see that Booth Tarkington's daughter died of pneumonia?" Grace asked. Without waiting for an answer, she went on, "how sad for him. I've read Penrod, of course, but I haven't had a chance to read his latest book." Chloe chuckled. "That Penrod - he's something else, isn't he? So much like Tom Sawyer!"

Grace said soberly, "I've been reading about the House of David trials in Grand Rapids. How anyone can fall for such drivel is beyond me!"

Hearing the jingle of a horse and wagon in the alley, Grace said, "Oh, good —the ice man is here." She retrieved thirty cents from the jar on the windowsill and met the workman at the back door. Grace gave the coins to the iceman. "Here, Sam—I should be able to catch up with last month's account by the end of the week."

He nodded and said, "I sure hope so, Miss Grace." In preparation, she'd emptied the pan of melted ice water underneath the icebox, and now she opened the door to receive the block of ice. With that, the family's cold food was safe for another few days.

An hour later, the pie and biscuits were ready, and as the aroma of sausages sizzling in sauerkraut reached her, Grace wrinkled her nose. She didn't love German cooking as much as the rest of her family, but her Papa insisted on it, saying it reminded him of home. While it was cooking, she had set up the ironing board and heated the iron on top of the stove.

This was only the latest in the long list of chores Grace had finished today. Up at 5am every morning to cook breakfast and see the twins off to school, she then had to dust and mop the whole house, do the daily laundry for five people, bake bread, scrape the ashes out of the fireplace, and generally keep the household going so that her parents could work. For Grace, it was a labor of love; her only regret was having to drop out of school. She tried to continue her education through books from the public library, but it was definitely a struggle.

"Hey, would you like to stay for dinner?" she asked. Chloe responded, "and eat your cooking instead of my own? Of course!" A few minutes later, they heard the front door open, and the raised voices of the twins, Franz and Frieda, Grace's two younger siblings, as they slung their books by the front door and burst into the kitchen. "The hordes have arrived!" Grace said.

# Chapter 2: Startling News

The next half hour was chaotic, as Grace kept one eye on supper, sprinkled starch water on the pile of aprons, started the ironing, and directed her brother and sister.

"Franz, do you still have arithmetic to finish up? Then sit here where I can keep an eye on you and start working. Frieda, take the silverware and go set the table. You know Papa likes to have dinner ready the moment he walks in the door."

Ignoring Frieda's whining, she handed her the silverware and gave her a gentle push in the direction of the dining room. Five minutes later, carrying the cast iron skillet in thick towels, she pushed against the swinging door with her hip and to see the silverware lying in a heap on the table. Frieda was nowhere to be seen.

Sighing in exasperation, she set down the hot dish and called for Chloe to bring the biscuits, and then went to the foot of the stairs to shout, "Frieda Ida Nora! Get down here pronto!" Chloe, coming in the swinging door, grinned and said, "Bringing out the big guns, are we?"

While the kitchen managed to be well-lit, with windows letting in the sun, the dining room was a study in darkness. Faded forest green wallpaper patterned with maroon scrolls would have been bad enough, but the dark green velvet curtains, always kept closed, made the room -- to Grace's eye -- suffocating. Even if the curtains had been open, the bushes outside the windows were overgrown and needed trimming. No amount of light from the gas chandelier helped relieve the gloom.

Grace made sure everything was on the table and checked the clock. Long practice enabled her to have everything ready when her parents got home. Her papa, Herman Dorsch, worked at the local Ford Motor plant, assembling motor cars, and her stepmother Maude worked as a garment cutter. Together they made enough money, as Maude said, "to keep body and soul together" but not enough for extra luxuries.

Mealtimes were never relaxing for Grace. Her parents were always occupied in complaining about the state of the world these days, the utter depravity of city youth, and the high prices of groceries. They had little energy or attention to spare for the twins, who took full advantage of that fact. While Grace was turning to ask Chloe a question, Franz pulled his sister's hair, hard. When she screeched in response, he turned an innocent face to his older sister as she warned, "Franz Friedrich, do that again and there'll be no pie for you! You're almost eleven years old, now act like it!"

Toward the end of dinner, as happened at least twice a week, Frieda reached for her glass of milk and knocked it over. As Grace rose to move plates out of the way and Chloe (who had younger siblings of her own) went to the kitchen for a dish towel, the doorbell rang. Franz leaped to his feet yelling, "I'll get it!" Frieda chased him to the front of the house, crying, "You always get there first! Let me answer it!" Grace and Chloe continued mopping until the table was set to rights again.

Franz came running back into the dining room, waving a letter in the air. "Special Delivery for Miss Grace Dorsch!" he announced. Three sets of hands reached for the letter, but Grace managed to pluck it out of Franz's hands moments before her parents got to him. Everyone sat down at the table again and waited with anticipation as

Grace reached for a clean table knife and slit open the letter. Frowning, she said, "This appears to be from an attorney." Reading aloud, she continued,

# Mr. Thomas Randall, Esquire
## Detroit    Mount Pleasant
## Traverse City

*Dear Miss Dorsch,*
*This letter is to inform you of a recent bequest left to you by the late Miss Edith Van Wagoner, distinguished professor at Central Michigan Normal School in Mount Pleasant. This concerns property of some value located in Benzie County, Michigan. Please come to my office in Detroit by May 1 to discuss the distribution of this bequest. No appointment necessary.*

*Sincerely,*
*Thomas Randall*

After a moment of stunned silence everyone started talking at once. In the same instant Frieda said, "I wonder what she left you?" and Franz said, "It could be a million dollars!" Papa muttered, "I bet it's a swindler", and then Mama raised her voice and said, "It appears I will have to take a day off to go with you. I can't spare the time, but you cannot go downtown unaccompanied. "

In response, Chloe volunteered, "Oh, Mrs. Dorsch, I can go with Grace - I've been downtown lots of times!" She leaned over to look at the letterhead. "His office is on Woodward, that will be easy enough to find." Mrs.

Dorsch's face cleared, and she replied, "Why, that would be very helpful and save me trouble. Thank you, Chloe."

Dismissing the matter, Grace slipped the letter into her apron pocket and rose to start clearing the table. Knowing everyone's answer already, she asked the room, "Who wants peach pie?" As she headed back into the kitchen Chloe followed her and suggested, "Let's go tomorrow morning, bright and early! I can't wait to find out what this is all about!" Grace shrugged. "Well, if I don't get my hopes up I won't be disappointed. I learned that the hard way."

Much later, in the upstairs bedroom, Maude looked at her husband and in a low voice said, "You should have told her years ago. What's going to happen when she discovers the truth?"

Shoulders sagging, Herman nodded in agreement, not willing to argue the point. Turning to the closet, he reached up and grabbed an old note box he had hidden on the top shelf long ago. Opening it, he looked through the few papers there: a death certificate, a marriage record, a couple of faded photos, and a brief obituary from the Detroit paper.

> DORSCH – Dec. 21, 1902, at residence, 14040 Rosemont. Charlotte, beloved wife of Hermann and mother of Grace, daughter of the late Dr. Marshall Roberts. Funeral from parlors of J. Sutton & Son, 4147 Trumbull Ave., Tuesday at 2pm. Benzie papers please copy.

His eyes went to the last line of the obituary, "Benzie papers please copy." Shaking his head, he put everything back in the box and put it back in its hiding place, making sure to pile more boxes on top of and in front of it.

Maude looked resigned. "I think we're about to lose Grace. I'll place a want ad for a housekeeper as soon as we know for sure."

Downstairs, in her tiny bedroom just off the kitchen, Grace was getting ready for bed. Nightgown on, clothes folded on the chair next to her bed, she crawled under the covers. It had taken her a little longer than usual to clean up the kitchen after dinner, so she wouldn't have as much time for reading before she needed to be asleep.

First, though, she leaned over and plucked the attorney's letter out of her apron pocket and read it again. Lingering over the words "a property of some value," Grace allowed herself to dream. Maybe it was an antique grandfather clock that she could sell to buy herself some books. She knew the million dollars that Franz had suggested was ridiculous, but she wouldn't mind inheriting fifty dollars. She'd taken a quick look at the atlas kept in the living room, so she knew where Benzie County was, and saw that it bordered Lake Michigan, which looked as big as the ocean. Putting the letter away and turning off her lamp, she fell asleep imagining herself walking in the sand without a care in the world.

# Chapter 3: The Will

The next morning, filled with anticipation, Chloe and Grace stepped off the trolley onto Woodward Avenue. Despite her voiced disbelief, Grace found that Chloe's excitement was infectious. It wasn't often that she was able to venture downtown, and it was always thrilling. They felt dwarfed by the tall red brick spires of First Presbyterian Church, and by the soaring square tower of St. John's Episcopal Church. Soon they were passing J.L. Hudson's (oh, for the funds to go shopping!), and Sander's Confectionery.

Using the letter as a reference, the two girls walked several blocks until they reached the office building. Pulling open the heavy front door, they marveled at the marble columns, tiled floor, and high ceilings of the lobby. "Here, his office is down this hallway," Chloe said, pointing to the right.

As Grace entered Mr. Randall's office, Chloe right behind her, the receptionist glanced up from her desk. She wore a starched shirtwaist and wire-rimmed glasses, with her hair in a tidy bun, making Grace feel gauche and disheveled. She gave her name, and the woman said, "I'll tell Mr. Randall you're here."

Coming back, she ushered the girls into Mr. Randall's office, a room lined with bookshelves and with a view of downtown Detroit. Mr. Randall, far from being the older white haired attorney Grace had imagined, was balding, rotund, and beaming at them.

Grace introduced herself and said, "I brought my friend Chloe with me," and Mr. Randall nodded and suggested, "for moral support, perhaps? Please, have a seat. Would either of you like coffee or tea? No? Well, then, shall we proceed?"

Taking a thick file from the top drawer of his desk, he continued. "As I mentioned in my letter to you, you are named as the beneficiary of Miss Edith Van Wagoner, who was a professor of English at Central Michigan Normal School in Mount Pleasant. Although I didn't know her personally, she had a reputation for warmth and humor, and demanded excellence from her students. I have here her last will and testament, dated three years ago. I'll read the pertinent parts:

*"I hereby give and bequeath to Grace Eleanor Dorsch my cottage located on Crystal Lake, in the village of Beulah, Benzie County, Michigan. The legal description is as follows:*

*A part of the west half of Lot 3 of Section 15, Township 26 North, range 15 West, described herewith:*

*Beginning at a point in the center of the North shore County Highway 503, 8 feet Northwesterly along center line of highway from the East side of above described parcel, thence North 38 deg. 52 min. East 246 feet, thence North 23 deg., 25 min. West 115.2 feet, thence South 38 deg. 52 min. West 276.5 feet, to center of*

*highway, thence South 31 deg. 55
min. West 140 feet, to water's edge of
Crystal Lake, thence South 58 deg. 05
min. East 100 feet along water's edge,
thence North 31 deg. 55 min. East to
place of beginning together with
beach and riparian rights, except
highway crossing same.*

*This bequest includes the cottage and all furnishings
and household items. I also have left in trust an amount
sufficient to support Grace for many years, to be given to
her at the rate of $25 each month. It is my wish that
Grace reside in this cottage for a full year, making use of
my extensive library to further her education, so that if
she wishes, she can follow my example and attend the
college of her choice. I further request that Grace not sell,
rent, trade or otherwise dispose of this property for five
years from the date of occupation."*

Mr. Randall added, "There is a codicil, written six
months after the original will, making provision in case
you couldn't be located. But of course, that no longer
applies." He looked up at Grace's open-mouthed
amazement. "I take it this is a surprise to you?" Grace
sputtered, speechless for a moment, and Chloe jumped in
with a torrent of questions.

"Where is Beulah? Why Grace? How did Miss Van
Wagoner know Grace?"

Mr. Randall replied, "Beulah is in the northwest part
of the state, situated near Lake Michigan, about an hour's
drive north of Manistee. As for the connection with Miss
Van Wagoner, I'm afraid I don't know the answer to that
question. My colleague took care of her legal affairs." He
continued, "I will be travelling north to my summer home

in Frankfort next Saturday; you are welcome to join me. Your train ticket, of course, will be paid for."

He went on to discuss particulars of what she should pack, adding that ample shopping was available in the nearby towns. "This is a resort area, so stores are well stocked to accommodate vacationers." He took a business card and handed it to Grace, telling her that he had a revolving account at J.L. Hudson's, and she should feel free to buy any necessities there before traveling north.

Mr. Randall's voice seemed to fade as Grace began imagining what this would mean for her future. A home of her own, new friends, time to read and study. The possibilities were endless. She was grateful for Chloe's presence, knowing that her friend would pick up whatever she missed. The phrase "extensive library" had caught her attention, and something in her heart blossomed at the thought of being able to read unencumbered by household chores and constant interruptions.

She was brought back to earth when Mr. Randall took another file folder out of his desk. Clearing his throat, he continued, "I thought perhaps you might be unfamiliar with the area, so I gathered some brochures for you. They do an admirable job of describing the local attractions."

Chloe, seeing that Grace was still dazed, took the folder, and standing, said, "Thank you so much for your time. I'll make sure Grace is at the Central Depot next Saturday morning."

# Chapter 4: Sodas and Shopping

Coming out of the building into bright April sunshine, Grace, lost in thought, almost missed a step. Chloe steadied her with a helping hand. "We don't have to be back at your house yet, let's stop at Sanders and have an ice cream soda."

Right around the corner was Sander's Parade of Sweets. Both girls had been here before, but it had been a long time since they were free to linger over an afternoon treat. Sitting at the counter and ordering their ice cream sodas, Chloe got out the folder and opened it. Out spilled several colorful brochures, proclaiming, "Michigan's Paradise!", "Visit the fair waters of Crystal Lake," "See the last stand of white pine in the state!" Their two heads bent over one paper, that showed a map of Benzie County, with Crystal Lake taking center stage. Beulah was at the southeastern end of the lake, Benzonia to the southwest, and Frankfort was further west, on Lake Michigan. Smaller towns were marked, too – Honor and Elberta, with arrows pointing north to Sleeping Bear sand dunes and south to Manistee.

Also included in the folder was a recent copy of the local newspaper, *The Benzie Banner*. From between the pages of one of the brochures slipped a faded photograph, of a white frame cottage surrounded by birch trees. On the back of the photograph was written in faint pencil: "Rustic cottage on Crystal Drive. Lamplight, kerosene stove and outside facilities combine to give a relaxing escape from busy city life."

Chloe interpreted, "That means an outhouse, probably with an outside pump as well. But from the looks of it, the beauty of your surroundings will more than make up for the inconvenience!" Grace agreed, remembering that it wasn't that long ago that her family had an outhouse at the bottom of the garden. And a kerosene stove sounded like a step up from the wood stove she dealt with at present.

Grace spoke for the first time since leaving Mr. Randall's office. "I can't believe this is happening! Who would bequeath me a cottage, so far away from everything I'm familiar with?"

Chloe, ever practical, answered, "I imagine you'll find out, sooner or later, who Miss Van Wagoner was, and how she knew about you. But for now, let's start making a list of what you'll need to pack." It didn't take long, for Grace did not own much. A few dresses, a sweater, her stockings, and shoes. More important, though, were her most treasured possessions: the two books she owned, and her mother's locket. Oh, and one or two of her favorite cookbooks. Now, with a kitchen all to herself, and no one else to cater to, she could cook and bake to her heart's content.

Walking on their way back to the trolley, Chloe stopped in the middle of the sidewalk and suggested, "I have a great idea! Let's stop in at Hudson's – I know you need new aprons, and you could use a new housedress as well!" When they reached the store Chloe led the way, having been there before. Grace was overwhelmed by the size of the store and the incredible array of household goods for sale.

Ending up in Women's Wear, Chloe helped Grace pick out two aprons, a housedress, and a new corset, as well as a lovely blue dress. "Just because you're going to a rustic area doesn't mean you shouldn't look nice!"

When they got to the sales counter with their arms full, Grace turned a stricken face to her friend. "If I come home with all these new things, my family will know I have money now!" Chloe thought for a moment and then asked the salesgirl, "Could we have these delivered to Beulah, in northern Michigan?" At her nod and reply, "Of course, Miss," Grace gave a sigh of relief and dictated, "Grace Dorsch, General Delivery, Beulah, Michigan," giving her Mr. Randall's card as payment.

# Chapter 5: Leaving Home

Since Grace was getting home later than she thought she'd be, the whole family was waiting for her in the front room. As she headed up the front steps the twins were hanging over the edge of the sofa, peering out the window. No sooner had she shut the door before they were at her side, tugging at her skirt for attention.

"Well?" Franz demanded, "What was it? Did you get a million dollars?" Herman and Maude were not far away, trying not to be obvious in their curiosity. Grace laughed. "Here, let's sit down and I'll tell you about it."

As the rest of her family listened with anticipation Grace went on, "It's still puzzling to me, and I can't help thinking it's been a mistake somehow, but Mr. Randall says someone has left me a cottage up near Manistee, in a tiny village called Beulah."

Maude and Herman exchanged a look. "Well, how fortunate. That must be worth some money, wouldn't you think?"

Grace dodged the question by saying, "I don't know," while thanking Miss Van Wagoner, whoever she was, for her foresight in requesting that she not sell the cottage for several years. Then she added, "Mr. Randall is leaving next week for his summer home in Frankfort and has tickets for me to accompany him."

Maude asked her, "Are you sure this isn't some kind of scheme to swindle you?" Grace laughed and retorted, "Swindle me out of what, exactly? From Mr. Randall's description the cottage is tiny and is a fair distance from the village." Maude continued, "Northern Michigan is a wilderness! And how will you live, without an income?"

Impish, Grace replied, "I can always hire out as a housekeeper, can't I? Mr. Randall told us Beulah is in the center of a popular resort area, so I'm sure there will be people needing household help!"

She continued to dismiss her parents' objections, ending with a spirited declaration, "I'm almost twenty-two years old now and it is high time I was out on my own. And it's not as if I'm going to the Sahara Desert – there will be plenty of people around to help me settle in. Now if you'll excuse me, I need to go start dinner."

The following day Grace corralled Franz and Frieda the moment they got home from school, bringing them into the kitchen for a lecture and some beginning lessons on housekeeping.

"It's time for you two to stop being such infants and start pulling your weight in this household. Our parents can't afford a full-time housekeeper, so you need to step in and help with the chores. Frieda, I'm going to be teaching you the basics of laundry and cooking. Franz, you can start by emptying the ashes from the wood stove and furnace and sweeping the front and back porch. Now let's get started - there's no time to waste!"

The next few days were a whirlwind for Grace, as she packed her small suitcase and tried to think of everything she might need to take on her journey up north. She spent most of her time in the kitchen, baking enough bread, rolls, pies, and cookies to last at least a week. She started Frieda doing basic laundry, hanging out the wash, and ironing, and began instructing Franz on other chores. Frieda turned out to be better at ironing than Grace and took a distinct satisfaction in turning the pile of wrinkled shirts and aprons into stacks of ironed linens. For his part, Franz took a decided shine to cooking, and Grace teased him about becoming a famous chef one day.

To her surprise, the children rose to the challenge without complaint, and Grace had a sudden insight into their previous behavior. They'd been acting up because they were bored and without any boundaries. Now with new responsibilities Franz and Frieda were indeed starting to grow up, working as a team rather than fighting with each other.

# Chapter 6: The Trip North

Stepping down from the trolley into the covered walkway of Detroit's Metro Station, Grace was struck by the cacophony of noise and movement around her. It was only a minute, though, until Mr. Randall appeared, and she felt a wave of relief.

Chloe said, "Here's your suitcase, now – don't forget to write! I'll haunt the mailbox until I hear from you! And remember – if you need me for any reason, just holler and I'll be on the next train." With that and a quick bear hug, Chloe turned and was soon lost in the crowd surging toward the trolley.

Mr. Randall took her suitcase. "I've got our tickets – we're taking the Pere Marquette to Grand Rapids and then the Ann Arbor north to Beulah. We should arrive there in the early evening." Handing their suitcases to the porter, he helped Grace up the steep couple of steps to the passenger car and led the way down the aisle to their seats. He placed his briefcase under the seat and Grace did the same with her satchel. Grace, happy to have the window seat, looked around her with delight. This was better than Christmas!

Mr. Randall, smiling, asked, "Is this your first train trip?" She replied, "Yes, it is. I've never even been outside the city limits."

With a loud screech the locomotive sounded a blast on its horn that Grace felt sure could be heard in Canada, right across the Detroit River. She clung to the edge of her seat and gazed at the scenery going past at a faster pace than she'd ever traveled before. Mr. Randall, having many years' experience traveling this route, took some papers from his briefcase and began reading.

Grace followed his lead and took her book out of her satchel and tried to read. But it was no use – she kept sneaking glances out the window at the passing scenery. Orchards of apple and pear trees, an occasional farmhouse, and now and then a small town, with a line of cars behind the stopping gate, all went by.

Her thoughts tumbled in her head, chasing after each other. Who would meet them in Beulah? If the cottage was furnished did that mean there were dishes and silverware, pots and pans? And what about food – would there be anything to eat until she could get to a shop? At that last thought, Grace realized she was in danger of her stomach growling and embarrassing her.

As if reading her mind, Mr. Randall replaced his papers in the briefcase and pulled out a package. "Mrs. Schmidt, my housekeeper, was so kind as to pack us a lunch." He gave her a wrapped sandwich that turned out to be roast beef between slices of crusty homemade bread. A bunch of plump red grapes appeared, along with still chilled bottles of Vernor's ginger ale. After they finished, and had changed trains in Grand Rapids, Mr. Randall brought out dessert: two pieces of Sanders chocolate bumpy cake in cardboard boxes, with forks and napkins.

Once she had finished eating, Grace felt much more relaxed and stopped worrying. "Do you know if Miss Van Wagoner grew up in Beulah?" Mr. Randall thought for a moment.

"No, I don't know, but I seem to remember hearing that she attended Benzonia Academy." At Grace's blank look, he explained. "The town of Benzonia is the next town up the hill from Beulah and was founded in 1860 by a group of Congregational ministers from Ohio. They made up the name: it's supposed to mean 'good air' or some such. The Academy never became a great success and closed a few years ago. You'll find that education is important in this part of the country."

Grace laughed and responded, "I'm so glad to hear that! To be honest, my parents aren't big on education; they value thrift and hard work more than anything else. In fact, when I was about twelve years old one of my teachers came to visit my father, to ask him if I could have extra study time at home. Papa chased her out of the house, roaring that an eighth-grade education was good enough for him, so it should be good enough for his daughter."

She smiled as she continued, "The next day I was called to the principal's office and told that I'd be given extra time during the school day to complete my work, so I wouldn't have to take any home." She shrugged. "Not that it helped - I had to drop out the next year anyway, because we couldn't afford a housekeeper anymore."

Mr. Randall hid his dismay at this cavalier dismissal of education and told her, "Well, with Miss Van Wagoner's personal library and more time to read and study, I'm sure you'll be caught up in no time. And be assured you'll have lots of support in the community."

As the afternoon wore on, Grace noticed the landscape starting to look different. Instead of flat farmland they were going through more hills, and the woods were thicker. Mr. Randall explained that they were traveling through the Manistee National Forest. Flashing in between the trees were glimpses of lakes and streams, and Grace thought she saw a white-tailed deer bounding into the forest. Truly, this landscape looked very different from downtown Detroit.

Mr. Randall had been wondering what possible connection this girl from Detroit could have with a college professor. He asked in a friendly tone, "So, tell me about yourself. Your last name sounds German – were your parents born in Germany?"

Grace responded, "My father was born in Germany and came to the U.S. about 1897. Then he married my mother. She died when I was a baby, and Papa married my stepmother Maude when I was about five. She came here from Canada. My younger brother and sister, Franz and Frieda, were born when I was ten, and I've taken care of them, and the house, since I dropped out of school. That way both Papa and Mama could work."

Mr. Randall said, "I'm wondering, if your Papa didn't know of Miss Van Wagoner, perhaps your mother is the connection there."

Grace replied, "I really don't know much about my mother at all. Her name was Lottie, and I have a locket with a small picture, but that's all I have."

As the train drew nearer to their destination, Grace spared a thought for her family she'd left behind. She felt a little guilty about leaving them, but the twins had mastered the basics of housekeeping, and Chloe had promised to stop in and check on them a couple of times a week. Grace resolved not to worry about them, and to enjoy this most unexpected gift.

# Chapter 7: Arrival

It was dusk when they finally pulled into the small depot at Beulah. Exciting as it was, the train trip had still been long and tiring and Grace was glad to be nearing the end of her journey. Mr. Randall, over her protests, carried her suitcase. After he helped her down the steps to the platform, he looked around and brightened as he spotted a horse and wagon waiting.

"Hey there, Fred – it's good to see you after a long day of traveling!" To Grace he said, "This is Fred Small, the owner of the local livery service and the town veterinarian." [2]As he helped Grace up into the wagon he introduced her, "Fred, this is Miss Grace Dorsch; she's taking up residence in Miss Van Wagoner's cottage, on the north shore." Fred nodded to Grace and told her that he'd picked up her box from Hudson's at the post office, "so's you'd have it with you at the beginning."

As Fred directed his horse down the main street of Beulah, which as Mr. Randall informed her, was named Benzie Boulevard, Grace looked around at the shops they were passing. Most of them were wood-framed, and some looked like they had false fronts on the second story. A few had balconies over the front porch, or awnings. The street reminded her of images of the wild west she'd seen on vaudeville shows.

---

[2] Fred Lapeer Small (1868-1959) lived in Beulah and worked as the town veterinarian and stable owner. His youngest son Lewis Small (b.1921) married my father's older sister Jane Reed.

"Going to Make a Drive?" *Benzie (MI) Record*, 20 May 1915, p.5, col. 5; PDF download, *Benzie Shores District*

Mr. Randall gestured to the lake behind the trees on his left and said, "Look at the sunset! The first of many for you, I am certain." Indeed, the sky was painted with hues of orange and pink and lavender, changing from moment to moment. He went on to tell her that the widowed lady living next door to the cottage had been taking care of it while it stood vacant, and he had sent her a message to have it ready for Grace.

As Fred turned the carriage onto Crystal Drive heading north, Mr. Randall kept up a running commentary on the cottages and their occupants. "Most of the resort cabins are on the south shore; the cabins and cottages on this side of Crystal Lake are owned by private families."

It wasn't long until Fred turned left off Crystal Drive and pulled up in front of a small, white-washed cottage. Beside the front door was a small carved wooden sign that said, "The Birches"; there was just enough light to see the small bush of fragrant white roses next to it.

"Here we are!" Mr. Randall helped Grace down from the carriage and retrieved her suitcase from the back. The door opened, letting out streams of welcoming light, and a woman's voice said,

"There you are! I was beginning to worry!" Mr. Randall introduced them, saying, "Grace, this is Hannah Thorpe. She lives next door with her son, and they've been taking care of the place." With that, he patted Grace's shoulder, told her that he was staying in Beulah overnight, and would be seeing her in the morning "to make sure you're settled in." He handed her the key ring he'd been carrying, waved to Hannah, and turned to leave.

Grace watched her last link to her old life in Detroit depart with Fred Small, and then turned to greet Hannah. Far from being the elderly, black-gowned widow she'd been imagining, Hannah was but a decade older than herself, with light brown hair gathered in a low bun and twinkling brown eyes. "You must be so tired after your long journey! I've fixed something for you to eat, but first let me show you your bedroom."

The hallway leading from the front door to the back of the house was tiny. To her left was the bedroom; Grace had a swift impression of the bed covers turned down waiting for her. Hannah placed Grace's suitcase on the cedar chest at the foot of the bed, and then showed her the way to the outhouse around the back corner of the house. When Grace came back, she splashed some cold water on her face from the bucket on the kitchen drainboard, then joined Hannah in the main living area. The room felt warm and cozy, lit by a kerosene lamp that threw shadows in the corners.

There was a small table on which was set out a plate of scones and a glass of milk. They sat down, and while Grace was eating Hannah kept up stream of inconsequential chatter about the area, recent events, and local people that Grace would get to know. At last she rose, and told her, "I'll be back tomorrow to show you around. I hope you sleep well tonight!" Grace walked with her to the front door, and then took up the lamp and made for the bedroom. It took no time at all to shed her clothes, put on her nightgown, and climb into the four-poster bed. Within moments she was asleep.

# Chapter 8: The First Morning

When the sunlight drifting across her eyelids grew too insistent to ignore, Grace opened her eyes and stretched, rested after the best night's sleep she could remember. No moment of strangeness for her; she knew where she was immediately and how she'd got there. Dressing hastily, she grabbed her shoes and made a quick trip to the outhouse. Coming back in the screened back porch, she quickly noted a laundry tub and wringer (more up to date than those she was using in Detroit), a stacked pile of firewood, and an old sofa covered with wool blankets. When she stepped back up into the kitchen, she stopped, astounded.

The previous evening, arriving late after a long day of travel with Mr. Randall, the interior of the cottage was shrouded in dim lamplight. By morning, however, it was a different story - the cottage was filled with sunlight. Ignoring for now the floor to ceiling bookshelves in one corner, she walked over to a closed door in the far corner of the main room and opened it. In the dim light Grace saw a set of wooden stairs leading up to the attic, resolved to explore that space later. Just outside the screened porch was a grassy lawn, sloping down to the lake. Resolving to explore the outside of the cottage after she fixed herself some breakfast, she turned back to the kitchen.

The kitchen, by itself, was a marvel. White painted walls with blue gingham curtains at the window overlooking the side yard would make any household chore lighter. There was an enamel sink bordered on each side with slightly sloping drainboards. In front of the sink was a blue painted stool, the perfect height for doing the dishes while gazing at the beauty of the outdoors. To the left of the sink were the ovens – two of them, on top of each other, and to the left of the ovens was a tiny four-burner stove with a brass teakettle at the ready. Underneath was a broad shelf which held various baking pans.

On the right side of the sink were the cupboards and shelves. Lined up on one shelf there was a row of wooden canisters labeled "Flour," "Sugar", "Cornmeal" and "Baking Powder". There were several smaller bottles of herbs and spices: basil, oregano, cinnamon, ginger. Grace opened the door of the icebox, which she saw was a little bigger than the one at home in Detroit. She saw a dish of butter, a pint of milk, a small pitcher of cream, a bowl of fresh eggs, and a pot of raspberry jam. She then opened the pie safe in the corner to find a loaf of bread and a plate of oatmeal cookies. Hannah thought of everything!

Starting to feel more and more at home, and marveling at her good fortune, Grace filled the kettle at the sink and set it to boil on the kerosene stove. Spooning tea into her cup, she cut a thick slice of bread, spread it with butter and jam, and ate it while waiting for her tea.

Cup of tea in hand, Grace opened the screen door and stepped out onto the wet grass. There was no wind, so Crystal Lake was smooth as glass - a bright blue glass, like nothing she'd ever seen before. Just ahead of her there was a tree. The bark was white and peeling off in places, and the leaves were silvery gray. Underneath the tree, facing the lake, there was a wooden bench.

Watching her steps across the lawn, Grace made her way to the bench and sat down. She was mesmerized by the lake – she had never seen a body of water like this. Her infrequent forays down to the Detroit riverfront with her father were full of noise: seagulls, trolley bells, the deep bellow of ships heading upriver to Bay City and St. Clair, and the constant sound of tires and taxi drivers.

Here was peace.

To Grace's amazement a bush at the far side of the yard started shaking. First a small fluffy dog and then a boy crawled out from under it. The boy, dark-haired and looking to be about 12, gave Grace a quick inscrutable glance, scooped up the dog and vanished through the trees to the house next door.

# Chapter 9: A Letter from the Past

Grace drank the last of her tea and returned to the cottage, reminding herself to add "new door mat" to her shopping list. Putting her cup in the sink, she turned with anticipation to the desk in the corner of the room, with the wall of floor to ceiling bookshelves behind it. Standing with her hands behind her back, almost afraid to touch anything, she scanned the shelves.

Many of the titles were old friends: *Understood Betsy, Anne of Green Gables, Tom Sawyer*, and *The Bears of Blue River*. There was a whole set of Charles Dickens, and she saw several books of poetry: Emily Dickinson, Tennyson, and Wordsworth. And over here was a well-used anthology of English literature.

Looking around the rest of the front room, she saw a fireplace with several lamps on the mantelpiece. There was a side table with a wind-up Victrola on it, and next to it were a stereopticon and set of slides. The floor was hardwood, with several rag rugs scattered around. She saw some antique framed needlepoint and on the small bookshelf in one corner were several photo albums.

Turning and looking at the desk, she saw a bulky object under a dust cover, which proved to be a typewriter. At one side was a thick Webster's Dictionary that she knew she would be using. Still feeling like an intruder, she sat down and started opening drawers. In the top middle drawer, there lay a sealed envelope, with her name "Grace" written on the front.

> *Dearest Grace,*
> *If you're reading this, it means my attorney has succeeded in tracking you down. Good for*

*him; he's been at it for a while. I imagine you were surprised at this inheritance.*

*My father built this cottage in 1875 and named it The Birches. It was passed down to me, and since I have no children of my own, I'm appointing you as my heir.*

*Your mother was my best friend; we were in school together as children, and at Benzonia Academy as young adults. That's where your parents met and fell in love. I had hoped that your mother would follow me to Central Michigan Normal School, but it was not to be. I knew and respected your father – he was a fine man. After he died and your mother left for Detroit and married Mr. Dorsch, we lost touch. I was sad to see her obituary in the local paper not long after that.*

*Please consider this cottage your new home. I hope you will love it as I have. I held you in my arms in this very room when you were only an hour old. It was my greatest sorrow when your mother took you away less than a year later and left in search of big city life.*

*She did leave some of her belongings with me; some of her books are on the shelf behind you, and the rest of what she stored here is upstairs in the attic.*

*As I mentioned in my will, it is my intent that you continue a course of self-study to further your education.*

*Beulah is a beautiful place to live, filled with good people who will become your friends. I know you will flourish here.*

*Much love,*
*Edith Van Wagoner*

Stunned, Grace raised her head from the letter to absorb the enormity of this message. A mixture of feelings and emotions descended: astonishment, anger, betrayal, and more than a hint of relief. How could her stepparents have kept this knowledge from her for so many years? Who else was in on the secret? Did she have any living relatives in this area – aunts, uncles, cousins? And finally she had an answer for why her blonde hair and blue eyes didn't resemble anyone else in her family, why she was so keen on further education, and why she didn't like German food.

Grace read the letter again, noting with astonishment that she had been born here. In a very real sense, she had come home to her place of beginning. She wished that Miss Van Wagoner had thought of mentioning her father's name. There had to be some way of finding out. Maybe the Academy in Benzonia had left records; she would ask Hannah about that.

However inviting the books on the shelves might be, they could wait. She had more urgent puzzles to solve.

# Chapter 10: Old Friends and New

Finishing up her lunch at the kitchen table, through the window Grace saw Mr. Randall drive up and park beside the cottage. By now he felt like an old friend, and she was glad to set aside the impact of her recent news, at least for a little while. She rose and met him at the back door, smiling at the sight of a familiar face.

"Well, how is it going? Are you settling in all right?" he asked, as he wiped his feet.

Grace beamed and gestured to the interior. "Here, I want to show you something!" She led him into the corner study area and showed him the shelves. "See – my own personal library!" He nodded. "Sure, and you'll have plenty to read over the next year or so."

He changed the subject. "I stopped by Central State Bank on my way here to get your first month's allowance." Handing her a bank book and $25 in cash, he smiled at her obvious delight. "Don't spend it all at once! If you need more for a major purchase, all you have to do is ask."

Head spinning, Grace decided to confide in him about the letter she'd found that morning. "Miss Van Wagoner left a letter for me in her desk. She said that I was born here, and that my father wasn't Herman Dorsch in Detroit!" Mr. Randall nodded, "Somehow that doesn't surprise me." He thought for a moment. "You know who might be able to help – someone told me that a librarian from the University of Michigan is vacationing up here this week. His name is

Mr. Gilbert Doane, and I believe you'll find him at the Northway Hotel. He will be well versed in research techniques."[3]

No sooner had Mr. Randall left than Grace saw Hannah walking across the backyard, carrying a basket over her arm. Walking next to her was the boy she'd seen in the bushes that morning, who had a wagging Pomeranian in his arms. Grace met them at the back door and welcomed them inside.

"Grace, this is my son, Ben. He's available to help with some of the chores that come with living on your own. I've asked him to pump a bucket of water for you every morning and keep your front doorway swept." Grace smiled at Ben, showing no hint that she'd seen him before, and at that Ben relaxed and smiled back. Hannah smiled and said, "And this is Parker House. She's named after the dinner rolls – light and fluffy!" They both started laughing and then Grace said, "I'm very glad to meet you both. I hope you'll bring Parker over to play sometimes."

Hannah placed the basket on the table and brought out a cherry pie, wrapped in wax paper. "Here, I brought you a welcoming present."

Grace said, "Well, after the morning I've had, this is a great time to have some!" She and Hannah brought out plates, cut three slices of pie, and sat down to enjoy it. "My word - this is delicious! Did you make this yourself?"

Hannah laughed in response. "Dear me, no - this is from the pie stand down the road. James and Dottie Kraker started it just last year, and they're doing a booming business! They call it The Cherry Hut."[4]

Ben went back outside to play, and Hannah rose from the table. "Follow me; I want to show you something. You could call it a feature of the cottage." She led the way to the front door and stopped on the front step. On the right side of the doorway was a post with a bell hanging from it that Grace had not noticed the night before. The bell

---

[3] Gilbert H. Doane (1897-1980) obtained his library degree in New York and was Assistant Librarian at the University of Michigan in Ann Arbor from 1922 to 1925. His book *Searching for Your Ancestors* was published in 1937.

[4] James and Dorothy Kraker bought several acres of land with established cherry orchards on the North Shore of Crystal Lake in 1921. They opened their roadside pie stand in 1922.

was sturdy cast-iron, weathered with years. Hannah pulled the rope gently and was rewarded with a mellow tone.

"Miss Van Wagoner had this school bell during her first teaching job, at the little one-room schoolhouse in Thompsonville. When she became a professor at the Normal School, she brought it home and hung it here. If you're ever in need of help, just ring the bell and it'll be heard for at least a mile."

After they went back inside, Hannah inquired, "So, tell me about your morning - it sounds like you've had some surprises?"

Grace fetched the letter from the desk and let Hannah read it. She looked at Grace and asked, "You know, I think I remember this! When were you born?" When Grace responded with "June 1901" Hannah nodded and said, "I came to Beulah every summer to visit my grandparents and I remember the lady, a widow, who was staying with Miss Van Wagoner, and the day she had her baby. So that means I've known you since you were born!"

Grace told her, "I want to find out more - no, I have to find out more! Mr. Randall suggested I ask Mr. Gilbert Doane for help. He's a librarian from the University of Michigan who's staying at the Northway Hotel."

Hannah rose and said, "There's no time like the present! I'll drive you to the village." Grace grabbed her satchel and put Miss Van Wagoner's letter, as well as Mr. Randall's letter, into it while Hannah went outside to tell Ben where they were going.

Grace followed Hannah to her home next door, to find a tidy yellow frame house with an older Model T parked in the driveway. Grace asked in surprise, "You can drive?"

Hannah laughed and said, "Yes, it's a very useful skill, let me tell you! If you like, I'll teach you how to drive, and when you get your license, you can borrow the car when you need to."


That same morning, two men looking much like the cartoon characters Mutt and Jeff were having coffee together at a table in the Whitman building in Benzonia. The lunch parlor there was a convenient place to meet and plan for their ongoing campaign to buy up local cottages around Crystal Lake and Platte Lake. On the table were spread the latest issues of the *Benzie Banner* and the *Record-Patriot*.

The taller man took up a paper and read aloud: "Two lots with cottages at Worden's Resort, all furnished with good boat included."

The short man nodded and read from his paper, "Twenty acres with half that cleared and four acres timber, close to Crystal Lake." They bent their heads together and began discussing the best (and cheapest) ways to obtain these and other properties like them, to 'rake in the dough.'

# Chapter 11: Ask a Librarian

Grace watched Hannah as she drove, switching gears like she'd done it all her life. They parked out the outskirts of Beulah, as Hannah said, "to let you see what's here in the village." As they walked down Benzie Boulevard, Hannah kept up a steady stream of commentary. Half listening, Grace kept looking to her right at the glimpses of Crystal Lake that appeared through the trees and between the houses.

"This is Tinkham's grocery store. I saw in the *Benzie Banner* yesterday that they have fresh oranges. And here is Percy Reed's shoe store."[5]

Special Sale on Ladies' and Children's Shoes

I am selling Ladies' Shoes, sizes 3 to 7 for per pair only

**$2.79**

These shoes are all regular $4 to $6 values and the number to be placed on sale is limited.

I also have on sale regular 75c to $1 Infants Shoes for 25c to 50c and and $1.50 first-step Infants Shoes at from 50c to 75c per pair. Seven styles for you to choose from.

**P. A. REED**

Harness and Shoe Repairing

Beulah, - - Michigan

"Special Sale," *Benzie (MI) Banner*, 5 January 1922, p.8, col. 1;

She looked down at Grace's feet, peeking beneath her ankle-length skirt. "If you're going to live here year-round, you'll want to get some sturdy boots for walking in the snow." She paused. "We get a lot of snow here; I'll make sure Ben keeps your walkway cleared." Hannah pointed out Fenton's Drug Store, the meat market, and Dr. Stone's office above Central State Bank. As they

---

[5] Percy A. Reed (1864-1955) was my great grandfather. He operated a shoe store on Benzie Boulevard; it is now the site of the Hungry Tummy Corner Pub.

walked past the bank, Grace made a mental note of their hours of operation.

When they reached the hotel, upon entering, Hannah pushed Grace forward and murmured, "Go ahead–ask for Mr. Doane." Behind them there was a cough, then a gentleman's voice saying, "Did I hear my name?" Grace turned to see a tall thin man with a kind face, just a few years older than herself. She blushed, and said, "I was told you might help me solve a puzzle."

"Well, I suppose that depends on the puzzle. But speaking as a librarian, I'm always glad to help."

Sitting down in the lobby area, Grace plunged into a semi-coherent explanation of how she inherited the cottage and came to know Mr. Randall and Hannah. She finished with, "I always thought I was born in Detroit, but Miss Van Wagoner's letter states that I was born here in Beulah! How can I find out for sure?"

Mr. Doane asked, "Your mother never told you this?" Grace shook her head at her omission. "I forgot to say she died when I was a baby. Or at least that's what I was told. Oh, dear," she almost wailed, "Now I don't know what to think!"

Mr. Doane patted her hand and reassured her. "My first piece of advice is to obtain your birth certificate. Do you see that long white building on the hill?" Grace nodded–it was gleaming white, two stories with several pillars along a lengthy porch. She'd meant to ask Hannah about it.

Mr. Doane continued. "That's the county courthouse. If you were born here in Beulah, there would be a record of it. It would be advisable to take both letters–from your attorney and from your mother's friend - as proof of your identity. They may not require it, but better go prepared."

Continuing to speak, he took a small notebook from his coat pocket. "If you will allow me, I can write my suggestions for further research." Grace nodded, relieved to have some expert guidance. She watched as Mr. Doane made a short list.

*Find your mother's death certificate*
*Find your parents' marriage record*
*Church records: baptism, marriage, burial*
*Cemetery records*
*Look for newspaper obituaries, here and in Detroit*

*Interview local residents who may have known your parents*
*Remember that records may be in neighboring counties*

He put a check mark by the first item, 'mother's death certificate' and said, "I think it will be faster if I obtain this for you. I have contacts in Lansing, including staff at the Michigan Department of Health. In fact, I can stop on my way home next week." He asked, "What was your mother's name?"

Grace replied, "Lottie. Lottie Dorsch. I don't know her maiden name."

Mr. Doane took a business card out of a case and handed it to Grace. "Here's my card – if you need any more help, or have additional questions, you can write to me here."

Just then Hannah reappeared, a basket over her arm, filled with the results of a quick trip to the meat market. "Are you about ready?" Grace nodded and thanked Mr. Doane again and joined Hannah in the car for the drive home. Hannah asked, "Have you ever had smoked fish?" When Grace shook her head Hannah told her, "Well, I got you some smoked whitefish and smoked trout for your dinner; I think you'll enjoy it."

When they arrived back at Hannah's home, Grace remembered the mailbox that Mr. Randall had pointed out to her. She went to check for mail, not expecting anything so soon after she'd arrived, and was startled at the lone envelope labeled 'OCUPANT'. Opening it, she read, "GET OUT OF THIS COTAGE NOW OR YOU WILL BE SORY" and then showed it to Hannah. Hannah laughed and dismissed it. "Investors are always trying to buy property on this side of the lake. I can't tell you how many shady characters I've had to turn away at my front door!"

# Chapter 12: The Birth Certificate

The following Monday morning found Grace staring up at the dazzling white façade of the courthouse, perched on a slight hill overlooking Crystal Lake. Two stories, with dormer windows on the roof and a covered porch running the length of the second floor, it was a graceful building. Grace and Hannah climbed the short flight of stairs and pulled open the front door.

Following the signs for the county clerk, they entered a small office with a counter and just enough standing room for the two of them. "Can I help you?" the young man behind the counter asked. Dressed in white shirt sleeves rolled up to his elbows and red suspenders, he was all business, until he smiled.

"Well – that is – I'm not exactly sure. I've always thought that I was born in Detroit, but recent events have pointed me towards Beulah as where my mother grew up. I guess I'm looking for my birth record."

"Give me your name and date of birth and I'll check the ledger," was the prompt response.

"Grace Eleanor Dorsch, June 21, 1901," Grace said. He disappeared into the back, between high wooden bookshelves lined with cloth-covered record books. Bringing one out, he opened it on the counter, flipped through some pages, and said, "Well, here's a birth record for a Grace Eleanor on that date, but the surname is not Dorsch, it's Warren." He examined the record. "Your father's first name is blurred, and here's a note next to it that says 'Deceased'". He turned the ledger around so Grace could see it in its entirety.

The ledger consisted of two pages for birth records; the left-hand page was headed "Child" and provided space for Date of Birth, Name

(If Any), Sex (and condition, such as Twin, Illegitimate, etc.) and Birthplace. The right most page held information about Parents: Full Name of Each, Residence, Birthplace, Occupation of Father, and Date of Record.

Studying it as the initial shock faded, she saw her name entered as Grace Eleanor Warren, and her birthplace as Beulah. Her parents were listed as ____ Warren and Charlotte Warren, who resided in Benzonia. Her father's birthplace was Manistee, while her mother's was Benzonia.

"Well," Grace straightened up and looked at the clerk behind the counter. "I guess that settles it. I was born here in Beulah!" Fishing Mr. Doane's list from her pocket, she said, "Could you check for my parents' marriage record, even if we don't know my father's first name?"

The clerk smiled as he took the Births ledger over to a side table. "I'll look that up for you in a moment. First let me type up this record so you'll have a copy." After he'd typed in the names on a standard form and stamped and signed it, he handed it to her. "My name is Allen Hopkins, by the way. Now I'll get the marriage register."

He brought another heavy ledger to the counter, this one bound in green, and as he opened it he explained, "This is a record of applications for marriage licenses for 1892 to 1902. You'll see there are two indexes in the front; one by the groom's surname and one by the bride's." He flipped to the page of grooms' surnames that began with "W" and ran his finger down the page. "I don't see it here," and seeing the look on Grace's face added, "that doesn't mean they weren't married. They could have gotten the license in a neighboring county - Manistee or Grand Traverse, for example."

Allen thought for a minute. "I've been to the Manistee courthouse several times. How about I take you there one day next week? If we do find the marriage license, we might want to visit the library or the newspaper office, as well." Grace accepted his offer, grateful to have added another friend to her growing circle of helpers. They agreed that Allen would call on her the following week and arrange a time for the trip south.

Driving home, Hannah agreed that going to Manistee was a good next step in Grace's search for answers. "The drive itself is very pretty, especially if he takes you by way of M-22. Inspiration Point is not to be missed!"

She continued, changing the subject, "You'll meet your neighbors along Crystal Drive sooner or later, but I wanted to tell you about Sheriff Miller ahead of time. He's two houses north of you, and while it is sometimes an advantage having the sheriff so close, there are drawbacks, too."

Grace asked, startled, "Like what?"

"For starters, it's his life's dream to catch a bootlegger in the act."

"Here – in Benzie County?"

Hannah laughed and admitted, "The most we ever see here is the occasional cache of cherry wine." She leaned closer to Grace and lowered her voice. "I have a couple of bottles hidden away; it's just the ticket if you've got a cough or sore throat." Hannah continued, "Most of the action is in Traverse City and the U.P., being so much closer to Canada. But as for the sheriff, 'hope springs eternal,' as the saying goes. Oh, and don't be alarmed if he acts suspicious when he meets you. He suspects everyone."

No sooner had Hannah dropped her off and gone home than an official looking Model A drew up to the cottage. Even without Hannah's description Grace recognized the figure of authority. With a paunch barely contained by the buttons of his uniform shirt, the man said, "Afternoon, ma'am. I'm Sheriff Ephraim Miller. Who do I have the pleasure of addressing?" He wasn't smiling and didn't seem pleased at all.

Grace stood straight as she answered, "I'm Grace Dorsch. I inherited this property from Professor Edith Van Wagoner."

A not-quite-sneer appeared on his face. "That so? Then why haven't I seen you before? And why didn't *Miss* Van Wagoner ever mention you?"

Grace replied, "As to the first question, I just arrived in Beulah not a week ago. And perhaps Professor Van Wagoner only confided in those whom she trusted; that is, her closest friends."

This reply didn't placate the sheriff one bit. "You got anyone can vouch for your identity?" Grace thought of Hannah or Allen but decided to aim higher. "Of course. My attorney, Mr. Thomas Randall, Esquire, has his summer home in Frankfort. He accompanied me here from Detroit. I'd be glad to give you his card." The sheriff took a step back, defeated for the moment. "No need. Dealt with him before.

Well, little lady, I will see you around." With that he got back in his car and roared off.

Grace shuddered. That parting shot was like hearing nails on a chalkboard. "Little lady!" Just wait until she told Hannah!

As Grace watched the sheriff drive away, she caught a glimpse of someone lurking in the shadows across Crystal Drive. The figure turned and ran before she could get a good look at them. Was someone watching her every move? It was a disquieting thought and Grace resolved to keep her doors locked even in such a rural area.

# Chapter 13: Letters Home

The next few days, Grace resolved, would be spent at home. She explored the other desk drawers and found a neat stack of writing paper, along with envelopes, stamps, and pen and ink. Chin in hand, she tried to think of how to describe to those at home in Detroit everything that had transpired in the last few days,

> *Dear Chloe,*
>
> *I made it to Beulah safe and sound, and the cottage is simply the berries! I can't wait for you to come visit, and marvel with me at my good fortune. The kitchen has a big icebox, and I arrived to find it well stocked with groceries by my next-door neighbor Hannah. She's been taking care of the cottage since the Miss Van Wagoner's death and has been helping me get acquainted with the area.*
>
> *My favorite part of the house is the "study", a corner of the main room with floor-to-ceiling bookshelves, filled with an entire library of good books. I don't think I can get through them all even if I live to be 80! Now that I have the time to read, I intend to make the most of it.*
> *The back porch of the cottage is screened, to keep the flies and mosquitoes out, and holds the washing machine and firewood. It also commands a wonderful view of Crystal Lake. I've*

never seen such a beautiful lake – I could sit gazing at it for hours.

The most surprising thing I've saved for last. There was a letter from Miss Van Wagoner waiting for me; she says that she and my mother were best friends growing up in Benzonia. What's more, she says my mother and father met at the local high school, Benzonia academy. So it would seem that Herman Dorsch is not my father at all, and I was born here in Beulah.

On Mr. Randall's suggestion I met with a university librarian named Gilbert Doane, who suggested I obtain my birth record. I went to the county courthouse yesterday and did so. My name at birth was Grace Eleanor Warren, and my mother's name was Charlotte. Hannah says she'll help me find out more about my parents, and I know Mr. Randall will help as well.

I'll write again next week

Grace

P.S. I'll never have to cook sauerkraut again!


Next, Grace wrote to her parents in Detroit:

Dear Papa and Mama,

I arrived safely in Beulah and am now settled in my little cottage. A widow named Hannah, lives next door and had the kitchen well stocked with groceries.

*There was a letter waiting for me here, from the professor who left me the cottage. She and my mother were best friends growing up, and she gave me some astonishing news regarding my earliest days. Evidently my mother and father met and married here, and after his death she took me and moved to Detroit.*

*You may appreciate what a shock it was to read such news. A librarian who is here on vacation is helping me to find out more about my birth family, and I am eager to find out if I have any relatives still in this area.*

*However, families are more than those related by blood. I am thankful for having grown up under your care and treasure the memories I will always hold dear.*

*I will write more next week,*

*Love to you all, Grace*

After some thought, she took another piece of paper and wrote a short letter to Mr. Doane, thanking him again for his help, telling him what she'd discovered about her birth record, and about the upcoming trip to Manistee. After she'd addressed all three letters, she resolved to put it all out of her mind for the moment and lose herself in a good book. Turning to the bookshelf, she picked *Understood Betsy*, an old favorite, and lay down on the sofa for a good read.

# Chapter 14: Exploring the Attic

On a rainy morning a few days later, sitting at what she was just beginning to think of as her desk, Grace couldn't concentrate on the book she was trying to read. *The Prince and the Pauper* by Mark Twain had been on her wish list for months, but now she was fretting about the anonymous letter in the mailbox, her unknown father, and wondering if she would get more unpleasant surprises as she researched. It was a relief when she heard the screen door bang open and Hannah's voice calling, "Yoo-hoo – are you at home?"

With a glance at Mark Twain that said, 'I'll see you later,' Grace went to meet Hannah and Ben. They were shaking out their raincoats and wiping their feet. Hannah wasted no time getting to the point of their visit. "Ben and I were wondering if you've been up in the attic yet."

Startled, Grace said, "No, I haven't. I've been so busy with everything...." She let her voice trail off as the enormity of her recent discovery overwhelmed her again. Hannah told her, "Well, Ben and I have been up there before, and a rainy day like this is perfect for exploring!"

Hannah leading the way, they walked over to an unobtrusive door set in the far corner of the main room. Hannah paused to light one of the lanterns on the mantelpiece and held it up to the open door to light the stairwell. Grace shook her head when Hannah motioned her to take the lead, and with that Ben charged ahead, climbing the five wooden stairs to the landing where the stairs made a sharp turn to the right. The top of the stairs opened into a wide attic room, stretching the entire length of the cottage. To their left was a small window overlooking Crystal Drive, and on the other side there were dormer windows overlooking the lake. Hannah hung the lantern on a hook in the rafters as Grace looked around her, amazed.

"There's room for a whole family to sleep up here!" she said aloud. Just ahead of her, underneath the gabled roof was a single bed covered with a faded quilt. Looking to her right, she walked over to the dormer window that overlooked Crystal Lake. On either side of the window was a single bed, both covered with yellow chenille bedspreads. And to the left was a row of three trunks, each with the initials "C.R.W." engraved on them. There was a smell of wood and old fabric, with the promise of treasures to discover.

Ben was on his knees in front of another open box that was full of old toys: hand-carved wooden trains, tin soldiers and rag dolls. "Now, Ben," reproved his mother, "Don't you think you should ask permission first?" Ben looked up at Grace with a silent appeal, and she laughed. "Of course, you can play with those! Just keep them up here and put them back in the box when you're done."

Very glad she'd chosen to wear one of her oldest housedresses, Grace knelt in front of one of the trunks. In the first trunk were stacks of magazines: *Vogue, Godey's Lady's Book*, several *Ladies Home Journal* and *McCall's*, with an occasional *Saturday Evening Post*. There was also a stack of paper dress patterns which looked interesting The second trunk held clothing that must have been her mother's. Grace resolved to look through the old-fashioned dresses and coats later and turned to the last trunk. It held the prize. Upon opening it, all Grace and Hannah saw was a fat bundle wrapped in brown tissue paper. When they lifted it out of the trunk and folded the paper back, a kaleidoscope of brilliant fabrics blinked up at them. "It's a crazy quilt," breathed Hannah.

# Chapter 15: The Crazy Quilt

With one accord, Grace re-wrapped the quilt and gathered it in her arms while Hannah shut the trunk lid. Standing, they headed toward the stairs and descended watching their steps. Once they were downstairs Grace moved her books from the coffee table and spread out the quilt. Mesmerized, they gazed in silence. In the years that the quilt had been packed away from the light, none of the fabrics had lost their brightness. Silk, satin, velvet and brocade patches in jewel tones of emerald, maroon, royal blue and bright green were bordered by decorative embroidery stitches. On some of the plainer fabrics there were embroidered birds and butterflies. When Grace, curious, lifted one corner of the quilt to examine the underside, she saw names written in black indelible ink: Florence Johnson, Emmeline Brooks, Temperance Crocker and others. She assumed that these were the names of the women who had worked on the quilt. It was truly a thing of beauty.

A thundering of footsteps was heard coming down the stairs from the attic, and Ben called, "Hey, Ma – you dropped something!" Breathless, he came up to them and handed Hannah a folded piece of paper. Hannah handed it to Grace, and when Grace opened it, a small round photo fell out. Ignoring that for the moment, she read the note to herself, and then aloud: "Dear Charlotte – best wishes to you on the occasion of your marriage". Signed, Y.P.S.C.E., Benzonia, July 1897."

Curious, Ben asked "What's Y.P.S.C.E. stand for?" Hannah replied, studying the note, "It's Young People's Society for Christian Endeavor." She handed it to Grace. "I think this must have been a group up at the Benzonia Congregational Church. If your parents were married there, they'll have a record of it." With that, Hannah picked up the photo. "I wonder whose photo this is?"

Grace took one look, made a sound like a sob, and rose to her feet. After a swift trip to the nightstand in her bedroom, Grace came back holding a locket on a chain. Sitting down again, she opened it to show Hannah. Although there were oval outlines meant for two photographs, there was only one there - of a young woman with light hair piled atop her head, wire-rimmed glasses, and a faint smile. The photo that Hannah was holding - of a young man, taken at the same time - was the same size and shape.

Grace fitted the photo into place. "I've always had this locket; the picture is of my mother. I wonder if this might be my father." After a moment she said, "I always wondered, deep down, why I didn't look like the rest of my family." Hannah smiled. "Well, now you know who you do look like – you can't deny the resemblance!"

Patting the quilt, Hannah asked Grace, "Would you like to go to church with us on Sunday? I think Pastor Fales would be glad to show us the marriage register." Grace hesitated for a moment and decided to take a chance in confiding to Hannah.

"Our family was never big on going to church. My stepmother went sometimes, and she let us decide if we wanted to go with her. But Papa always stayed home." Feeling almost ashamed, in a lower voice she said, "I'm not sure he even believes in God."

Hannah's response was reassuring. "Well, no one is going to quiz you about your beliefs. And if you're not familiar with the hymns and readings, they'll chalk it up to you being in a new place." Grace nodded. "In that case, yes, I'd love to go with you." Hannah rose from the davenport and told her, "Church starts at 10:30, so I'll pick you up about 9:45." To Ben, she said, "Let's be getting home; it's almost time for dinner."

# Chapter 16: The Photo Albums

Over the next few days, as Grace waited for Sunday to arrive, she busied herself in and around the cottage. On fine mornings she would take her tea out to the bench and sit looking at the lake, thinking of all that had happened. Then she spent some time in the long-neglected garden, pulling up weeds and identifying several of the spring flowers, such as trillium, spring beauty, hepatica, and bloodroot. Although she had never seen these before coming to Beulah, there was a book on Michigan wildflowers on her shelves, as well as a couple of seed & bulb catalogs. At the edge of the garden, she thought she saw several raspberry canes, and there was a row of five rosebushes underneath the porch windows.

One morning when she felt the water was warm enough, Grace took off her shoes and went wading in Crystal Lake. To her amazement, the water was clear as could be, and she could see every detail of the smooth stones on the bottom. She looked to the southeast and could make out the village of Beulah. In between, several cottages had docks  built out onto the lake, some with rowboats tied up to them.

Inside, Grace busied herself in the kitchen, trying out new recipes. Although she was trying to be careful with her month's allowance, she couldn't resist subscribing to *Ladies Home Journal*. Ben turned out to be a willing taster for her concoctions; his favorites were the oatmeal cookies with the surprise addition of dried cherries. In one of the kitchen cupboards she found a long wooden recipe box, full of recipes in an elegant but clear longhand. Soon she was adding her own.

One morning as she was working in the kitchen there was a knock at the front door. Wiping her hands on her apron, she went to answer it. Upon opening the door Grace told herself sternly, "Don't laugh!" because the two men on the doorstep looked exactly like Mutt and Jeff come to life. The taller man held out his card and began what sounded like a well-practiced spiel. "Good morning, miss. We are inquiring as to whether you would be interested in selling your beautiful home for a bountiful consideration?" Without thinking twice, she answered, "This house is not for sale!" and shut the door in their faces.

When she wasn't gardening or cooking, Grace continued to explore the cottage. Opening the cedar chest at the foot of her bed she found several blankets and old-fashioned quilts. And on the Saturday night before church, she took the stack of photo albums from the small shelf next to the fireplace and carried them to the kitchen table.

One of the albums was filled with photos taken at Benzonia Academy. Grace studied the groups of graduating classes gathered on the steps of a big brick house. There were several smaller groups of women, dressed all in white wearing sprigs of lily of the valley at their shoulders. Another album's leather cover was embossed with a lighthouse and filled with what appeared to be pictures of summer camping. Groups of women in dark skirts and white shirts sprawling on the ground under the trees were labeled, "Fun at Camp Wequetonsing, 1890," and underneath other pictures of cottages near Crystal Lake were written "Congregational Summer Assembly."

The album that Grace lingered over, though, was the largest and heaviest. Covered in heavy maroon velvet, there was an oval portrait of a small girl on the cover and written on the inside were the same initials as on the trunks upstairs: C.R.W. Grace was sure this photo album had belonged to her mother. As she paged through it, looking at the formal portraits, she was frustrated by the fact that none of them were labeled. She even took a few of them out of the album to check the backs.

She paused at a wedding portrait, and judging by the two images in her locket they were of her mother and father. Her mother was dressed in a light-colored gown trimmed in lace and carrying a small bouquet of roses. Her father, in a dark suit, was seated in a chair next to her, holding his hat on his lap. Scattered on the floor were what seemed to be rose petals, and the card framing the photo was stamped at the bottom, "Benzonia, Michigan". On the facing page was a photograph of her parents in their wedding finery in front of a fireplace decorated with strands of flowers with a potted palm tree at either side. In the flickering of the lamplight, they seemed to be looking right at her.

Past her usual bedtime, Grace closed the album and carried the lamp to her bedroom, wondering what new discoveries awaited at church.

# Chapter 17: Sunday Morning

That Sunday, as Hannah shifted to the lowest gear in preparation for climbing up the steep hill to Benzonia she commented, "They're just getting started on paving the roads in Frankfort; I hope Crystal Drive will be next." Grace nodded, hanging onto her hat and looking around her at the scenery. In the back seat Ben tapped her shoulder and said, "Look behind us, Miss Grace!" When she turned and looked over her shoulder, there was Crystal Lake shimmering amid the trees before it disappeared from view.

At the top of the hill they entered the town of Benzonia. As they passed a large red brick building on the left, Hannah pointed. "That's the Mills House; it's the last remaining building of Benzonia Academy. It's been vacant since the Academy closed, but there's talk of turning it into the town library." Grace recognized it from the photo album of graduations at the Academy. Soon after that Hannah turned right onto Traverse Avenue, and they were at the church.

It was a simple white frame church with a spire, like many other small churches across the Midwest. To Grace's eye, it had more simplicity and serenity than any of the huge churches in Detroit.

Much to her surprise, Grace felt comfortable in the church service. Hannah helped her find the hymns, and though she wasn't familiar with any of them, she could usually sing along after the first couple of verses. One of the hymns had a phrase that resonated with her: "our shelter, He, amid the flood of mortal ills prevailing." She was also astonished to see Sheriff Miller in the choir, singing a fine baritone.

After the service Hannah introduced her to Reverend Ira Fales, telling him that Grace had inherited Miss Van Wagoner's cottage on Crystal Lake. Rev. Fales shook Grace's hand. "Welcome to our little community – I hope you will soon feel at home here." Grace gathered up her courage and asked about seeing the church registers, explaining that she thought her parents had married here. "Of course, of course – come this way to the church office."[6]

In the office, Rev. Fales pulled down a red-bound ledger from a high shelf and asked, "When were your parents married? July 1897? Well, then, let's see if it's here." He turned the fragile pages until he came to 1897 and ran his finger down the columns. "Ah, yes, here we are!" Eagerly, Grace and Hannah bent to look at the entry. There it was: Edward Warren and Charlotte Roberts, married on July 14, 1897, by Rev. H.S. Mills.[7] Hannah leaned over and pointed out something Grace had missed at first glance. "Look, Edith Van Wagoner was one of the witnesses!"

As Rev. Fales copied the information for Grace and then closed the ledger to replace it on the shelf, Hannah thought to ask, "Would there be a burial record for Grace's father? We think he died in 1900 or 1901."

"Let me take a look," was the response, and soon another ledger was placed on the table. Rev. Fales turned the pages, looking at the entries in spidery handwriting. "Here it is: Edward A. Warren, died in Manistee on March 14, 1901. It says he drowned – how sad." He straightened up and told them, "This week while I'm here in my office I'll check through the file of old funeral sermons. Most of Rev. Mills's sermons were preserved." He thought for a moment and added, "You might check in Manistee for his death record, and for an obituary or death notice in the newspaper."

Grace had been thinking about church records while Rev. Fales replaced the ledger. Hesitantly she asked, "I was born here in Beulah. Could we look for a baptismal record for me?" Hannah looked at her in admiration, and Rev. Fales nodded and went to retrieve a different ledger. After carefully scanning several pages in June and July of 1901, they found the record.

---

[6] Rev. Ira D. Fales (1883-1965) was pastor of Benzonia Congregational Church from 1921 to 1927.

[7] Rev. Harlow Spencer Mills (1846-1931) was the pastor of Benzonia Congregational Church from 1896 to 1916.

"August 18, 1901," Hannah read aloud. Then she pointed out what Grace had already seen. "Look, Edith Van Wagoner and Charles Roberts are listed as your godparents!" Grace was filled with happiness to see a connection, however tenuous, with her benefactor.

"I wonder if Charles Roberts was an uncle or other relative on your mother's side?" Hannah wondered. Grace wondered, too, and resolved to discover the answer.

# Chapter 18: A Trip to Manistee

Hannah had noticed, even if Grace pretended not to, that Allen Hopkins was carrying a torch for Grace, stopping by The Birches several times a week. Grace found that far from being lonely or bored, her life was full and interesting. She and Allen had finally been able to schedule a day trip to Manistee, and the previous afternoon she crossed Crystal Drive to check her mailbox. She was delighted to see a letter from the University of Michigan addressed in Gilbert Doane's handwriting. Opening it, she found her mother's death certificate along with a short note from Mr. Doane.

Bracing herself for what she was about to learn about her mother's death, Grace went back into the cottage and sank down at the table to read. The death certificate, issued by the state of Michigan, was for Charlotte Dorsch, who died in her home at 14040 Rosemont in Detroit on December 21, 1902. Grace gasped as the full meaning of that date sank in. She had been eighteen months old, and her mother had died on Papa's birthday, four days before Christmas.

After a few minutes spent with her head in her hands, realizing why her Papa had always been stern and unsmiling, she wiped away tears and continued studying the certificate. Her mother's parents' names were Marsh Roberts and Eleanor (last name unknown), both born in Michigan. Charlotte's cause of death was recorded as "peritonitis following ruptured appendix." Underneath that the doctor had written, "no doctor in attendance, just a C.S.P." Underneath that, in a different hand, was scrawled, "patient refused medical attention." The line for informant was signed by Herman Dorsch. Puzzled by the last couple of notes, Grace placed the document in the folder she'd started, to hold all the information she was finding.

For the first time Grace was uncertain about any more exploration of her family history. Although her mother's death days before Christmas and on her Papa's birthday was bad enough, what further bad news awaited just out of sight? Were there murderers in her family tree? Prostitutes? Bums? Bootleggers? At that last thought her heart lightened a little, and she decided to ignore her pessimism and hope for good things. Perhaps she had unknown relatives living in the area. Or maybe she would find out where she got her love of reading and thirst for education, as well as her blonde hair.

The day for their trip to Manistee dawned fine and clear. Grace locked the front door and climbed into Allen's Packard, dressed in her usual traveling costume of duster with straw hat and veil. As he started the motor, Allen explained that he would be driving straight to Manistee on M-11 but would be coming back via "the scenic route," a somewhat longer drive that hugged the shoreline of Lake Michigan. As they drove on Crystal Drive's dirt road toward Beulah, Allen gestured to a cabin set back from the road on the hillside overlooking the lake. "That's where I live. My folks own this cabin as well as their home in Frankfort, and I'm the caretaker. It benefits all of us – I get a place to live, and they get someone taking care of it!"

After an hour-long drive on bumpy but paved roads, Allen pulled up in front of the Manistee courthouse. As they climbed the cement steps to the imposing red brick building, Grace couldn't help comparing it to the simple beauty of the courthouse in Beulah. They made their way to the clerk's office, where Allen introduced her to his friend Michael, who was helping people at the counter. Grace, consulting her notes, asked first for her parents' marriage record. Since she had the exact date – July 14, 1897 – he was able to pull down the correct register and start looking through it.

He explained as he turned the pages, "These records are arranged by year, and then in batches by town or village. Here's Arcadia, Bear Lake, Pleasanton, Onekama, Filer.... ah, here we are, Manistee." Soon he found the application for the marriage license for Edward A. Warren and Charlotte E. Roberts, dated July 12, 1897. Grace was glad to have found the record, but disappointed that it didn't name the parents of the bride and groom.

Grace handed the typed copy to Allen to place in her folder and asked the clerk to look for her father's death record, on March 14, 1901. That record was easy to find, and after the clerk had typed it up, she stood back from the counter and examined it. It stated her father's name as Edward A. Warren, date of birth 1873, cause of death "drowned" and names of his parents were Abijah Warren and Julia (last name unknown), both born in Massachusetts. The cemetery was "Oak Grove" in Manistee.

Allen, reading over her shoulder, pointed to the cemetery name and suggested, "Why don't we visit the cemetery next. I'll ask directions." There was a lull in the clerk's office, and Allen asked Michael for directions to Oak Grove. After Michael had drawn a detailed map he added, "You might want to visit S.C. Thompson's real estate office over on Engelman Street. He used to be editor of the *Manistee Advantage*, and what he doesn't know about area newspapers isn't worth knowing!"[8]

---

[8] Stacy Clay Thompson (1856-1944) lived in Manistee most of his adult life. He was a newspaper printer and editor, realtor and land speculator.

# Chapter 19: Visit to an Old Timer

It wasn't long before Allen and Grace drove through the gates of Oak Grove cemetery, and soon they saw a large marble monument just off the gravel road, with the name "Warren" on it. Getting out of the car and walking toward it on the freshly trimmed grass, they saw below the name, "Home is the sailor, home from the sea". After a few minutes of searching, Grace found her father's gravestone and sank down to her knees before it. Blinking back tears, she managed to read,

Edward A. Warren
Died March 14, 1901
John 15:13
Greater Love Hath No Man

Allen came up and put a comforting hand on her shoulder. She asked furiously, "How can I be so sad about someone I never knew?"

Allen responded, "Because you never got the chance to know him." He studied the inscription before telling Grace, "Come over here – I think I found your grandfather."

On the other side of the Warren monument was another stone. This one had the name "Abijah Warren" engraved on it. There were no dates, but there was a short inscription:

Sunset and evening star,
And one clear call for me

Grace said, "That's beautiful – it sounds like part of a poem."

Allen coughed and stood straight as he recited,

*Sunset and evening star,*
*And one clear call for me!*
*And may there be no moaning of the bar,*
*When I put out to sea,*

*But such a tide as moving seems asleep,*
*Too full for sound and foam,*
*When that which drew from out the boundless deep*
*Turns again home.*

*Twilight and evening bell,*
*And after that the dark!*
*And may there be no sadness of farewell,*
*When I embark;*

*For tho' from out our bourne of Time and Place*
*The flood may bear me far,*
*I hope to see my Pilot face to face*
*When I have crost the bar.*

After a moment he added, "I memorized that for a school recital when I was twelve. It's by Alfred, Lord Tennyson." He patted her shoulder. "Come on, I think it's time to visit S.C. Thompson and see if we can find an obituary for your father."

Half an hour later Allen and Grace were sitting across a polished oak desk from Mr. Thompson, who was every bit as stately as Allen's friend had described him. He was leaning forward listening intently as Grace told him about finding her father's death certificate. At its conclusion he rose. "You've come to the right place. Follow me." As he walked toward a storage room he explained, "I was indeed the editor of the *Advantage* for several years. During that time, I made a habit of collecting a copy of every daily paper in Manistee. At one point we had four papers published here: the *Advantage*, the *Broadaxe*, the *Times-Sentinel*, and the *Standard*. It should be easy enough to find an obituary for your father."

In the storeroom Grace was astonished to find shelves of folded newspapers; each shelf was labeled with the title and year. Asking her for the date again, Mr. Thompson pulled out a newspaper from each of two different stacks. "Let's start with these." As he unfolded the paper, they all saw there would be no need to leaf through it; Edward Warren's death was front page news.

### *Dies Saving Girl*
*Edward A. Warren of Benzonia*
*Drowned Yesterday.*
*while saving the life of 4-year-old girl.*

*His final act showed unusual heroism. Anna Becker and her family of Onekama were picnicking off Orchard Beach when the child waded out too far into the waves and was heard screaming. Regarding not his own safety, Mr. Warren plunged into the harrowing deep and grabbed her, handing her off to another rescuer before perishing.*

*Area residents will recall that Mr. Warren grew to adulthood in Manistee, the son of ship captain Abijah Warren. Edward Warren attended Benzonia Academy and was planning to apply to Oberlin College in Ohio to study for the ministry.*

*Funeral services will be held at Benzonia Congregational Church Saturday next at 10am. Interment to follow in the Warren family plot at Oak Grove Cemetery, Manistee.*

*Edward Warren is survived by his widow, Charlotte, and a host of friends who mourn his passing.*

The other three newspapers in publication at the time offered similar articles, with some differences. One of them named the rescued child Maria Beck, and another paper did not mention Edward's widow but stated he was survived by his elderly father and widowed older sister.

After copying the articles with paper and pen, making sure to note the title, date, and page number of each, Grace straightened up, feeling a little overwhelmed. Allen stood beside her in silent sympathy while Mr. Thompson folded the papers and stowed them back on the shelves. He turned and said, "Now, to happier times! Do you have a date for your parents' marriage?" When Grace told him, "July 14, 1897," he began searching for and then pulling out newspapers.

# Chapter 20: Inspiration Point

Again, they bent over the paper as Mr. Thompson carefully turned the pages. On the society page, bordered in fancy scrollwork, they read:

### *A Pretty Wedding in Benzonia*
### *Warren-Roberts Rites Solemnized*

*Last Saturday saw a very pretty wedding as Charlotte Roberts and Edward Warren were united in marriage at the home of the bride's father, Dr. Marshall Roberts of Benzonia. Pastor H.S. Mills of the local Congregational Church officiated before a gathering of close family and friends.*

*The bride was gowned in cream satin trimmed in ecru lace at the waist, sleeves, and hem, and carried a small bouquet of fragrant white roses. She was given away by her father and attended by Miss Edith Van Wagoner, here from Mount Pleasant, who wore light blue silk covered with blue organdy.*

*The home was beautifully decorated with palms, sweet peas and carnations, which lent a sweet fragrance to the air. Out of town guests included the bride's brother, Charles Roberts, here from Sacramento, California, and the groom's maternal grandparents, here from Rochester, New York.*

*The wedding couple received several
pretty and useful gifts, which were displayed
on a side table in the dining room. A handsome
collation was served, which included a
delicious wedding cake baked by the groom's
sister, Mrs. Phoebe Strickland.*

*After a wedding trip to the Upper
Peninsula the happy couple will be at home in
Benzonia.*

After copying this announcement, Grace asked Mr. Thompson, "I don't know if the Manistee papers would carry my mother's obituary, because she died in Detroit, but do you suppose we could look?" A search of all four newspapers for an obituary for Charlotte Dorsch in the week following December 21, 1902, failed to turn up any mention of her death. Mr. Thompson suggested, "Since she was originally from Benzonia, I would suggest checking the newspapers there."

Thanking Mr. Thompson and promising to keep in touch, Grace followed Allen out to the car. He helped her in and said, "I think it's time we had a change of scenery." Taking a different road north out of Manistee, Grace soon noticed that the road was starting to climb. To her left, through the occasional gap in the trees, she saw the horizon. She knew from the maps she'd seen that on that side lay Lake Michigan.

Allen pulled into the parking area at the side of the road and came around to Grace's side to help her out of the car. "This is Inspiration Point," he said. "It's the highest point on this side of Lake Michigan." He took her hand and they started climbing up the grassy hill, following a narrow trail. "Now Crystal Lake is nice, this view is the bee's knees!"

Watching her feet and breathing hard as she climbed, Grace wondered what on earth would possess someone to describe Crystal Lake as merely "nice". Coming to the top at last, glad to be able to catch her breath, she raised her head and stopped breathing again. Before them spread Lake Michigan in all its summer glory:

shimmering many hues of blues and greens, with a few clouds in the sky. Mesmerized, she thought she would never tire of the view.

There was a slight wind and the sound of the waves breaking on the sand far below them reached their ears. A single hawk was gliding above them. Allen pointed to the horizon. "Do you see that steamer out there? It might be a car ferry from Frankfort, on its way to Minneapolis or Chicago." He paused and added, "Sailing on the Great Lakes can be dangerous and difficult. Big storms can appear without a moment's notice, and in winter they've got snow and ice to contend with."

Then he pointed to the north. "Do you see that sand dune? The Indians called it Sleeping Bear, and there's a story behind that name. The legend goes that a mama bear and her two cubs were swimming in Lake Michigan when the cubs got tired and drowned. The Great Spirit turned them into the Manitou Islands. Mama bear headed back to shore and lay down to keep watch over them. It's a gorgeous spot; I'll take you there someday."

Allen said, "You know, after everything we've found out today, I imagine you're a little overwhelmed. Looking at this view always makes me think of my favorite verse from scripture: 'Be still and know that I am God.'" After a few more moments of silence, they turned and made their way back down the hill to the car.

# Chapter 21: An Ominous Note

On their way back to Beulah, Allen shouted over the noise of the motor, "My parents want to meet you – they've invited you for dinner after church on Sunday." Grace gulped and nodded because she sensed this would be an important occasion. Allen had already told her that his parents were John and Margaret Hopkins, who lived in a stately home in Frankfort. His mother was interested in genealogy and would be glad to help Grace in her quest to find more about her parents.

Walking alone into the cottage after Allen dropped her off, Grace was alarmed to hear the crunch of broken glass as she walked into the kitchen. The window over the sink was broken, and on the floor was a big rock about the size of her fist with a note tied around it. Unwrapping it, she saw the words "GET OUT" in the same hand that wrote the anonymous missive she'd received in the mail. Feeling unsettled, Grace went to get the broom and dustpan and set the note on the kitchen counter, to show Hannah later.

Moments after she started sweeping up the glass, Hannah came in the back door. "How was your trip to - wait, Grace – what happened here?"

"Well, I guess someone doesn't like me living here. See what I found on the floor when I walked in a few minutes ago?" She handed the rock and note to Hannah, who told her firmly to stop sweeping, "the sheriff will want to see this!"

Grace protested, "Don't you think it's those Mutt and Jeff characters, or someone like them trying to force me out?" Hannah looked at her. "Do you think they'd damage property they're trying to buy?" With that, Grace gave in, and agreed to drive with Hannah into Beulah to report the incident.

Sheriff Miller followed them back to the cottage from his Beulah office, and carefully surveyed the ground outside the kitchen window. "There are no footprints here, the weather's been so dry lately. You said this handwriting looked familiar?" With that, Grace had to confess that she'd thrown away the anonymous note, not thinking there would be any more.

The next morning Sheriff Miller was making his usual patrol in his car when he spotted the two real estate investors sitting outside a café. Getting out of his vehicle, he lumbered up to them. "Okay, boys – game's up. Time to pack your bags and leave town. The harassment you've been dishing out has gone too far." The two men protested, but not very hard, having halfway expected this response. They got to their feet and headed to the Northway hotel to pack their bags. The sheriff took the precaution of following them and a short time later had the satisfaction of seeing them off on the 5pm train to Grand Rapids.

Then, after canvassing up and down Crystal Drive to see if anyone else had received the same threats, the sheriff returned to The Birches. By then Grace and Hannah had cleaned up the damage, and Allen had stopped by and been dispatched to get new glass for the window. "I don't think you'll be bothered again, Miss Dorsch," the sheriff told her. "Be sure to keep your doors and windows locked." She just looked at him. "Sheriff Miller, I'm from Detroit. I always keep my doors and windows locked!"

After the sheriff left and Hannah went home, Allen and Grace continued discussing the incident. "Somehow, I think a rock through your window is more of a personal threat than wanting to buy the cottage would warrant," Allen told her. She had to agree. Although the two investors had been spotted talking to several neighbors up and down Crystal Drive, no one else had had a rock through the window or any threatening messages.

The following morning, Ben was up early, having made an important decision. When his mother came into the kitchen to start breakfast before Ben had to leave for school, he said, "Mama, I decided something last night. I want to give Parker to Miss Grace. She needs a guard dog." Hannah put down the bowl of eggs she'd been scrambling and turned to face him, surprised. "Ben, are you sure?" Resolute, he nodded. Glancing at the clock, she returned to making breakfast and said, "All right, we'll go see her after you get home this afternoon."

Grace was at her desk, trying (and failing) to concentrate on Shakespeare's sonnets when she was surprised to see Hannah and Ben walk in, accompanied by Parker House. Hannah was carrying a couple of bowls, and a dog bed and Ben was lugging a sack over his shoulder that was labeled "Battle Creek Dog Food Co." Grace stood up and then bent over to greet Parker, who was wagging to beat the band. She looked at Ben and Hannah, already guessing the answer. "What's all this?"

Ben said, "You need a guard dog, so I'm giving you Parker House."

Grace's immediate reaction was to refuse the offer, but she turned toward Hannah, who gave her a slight nod. Grace looked at Ben again. "How very kind and thoughtful of you! I will accept, on two conditions: that you come over to visit us every day, and that Parker goes back to your house after this crisis is over." This arrangement satisfied everyone, and so Parker's bowls were set in a corner of the kitchen, and her dog bed by the side of the desk.

That night, after Grace had let Parker out for her evening run, she debated on where Parker would sleep. Having no idea where the dog slept at Ben's house, she decided it was up to her to decide. Getting ready for bed and climbing in, she patted the covers, admitting to herself that Parker's presence was comforting. "Come on, Parker – you get to sleep with me, at least for the time being." Parker needed no further encouragement and jumped up and snuggled next to Grace, and soon they were both asleep.

# Chapter 21: John and Margaret Hopkins

On Sunday morning Grace dressed with care, thankful for the impromptu shopping trip at Hudson's in Detroit. That seemed so long ago! She gazed in the mirror and saw that the blue paneled crepe was crisp and fresh and complimented her blonde hair and blue eyes. She gave her corset a tug, and tucked the folder with the information she was collecting into her handbag.

After church, Rev. Fales pulled Grace aside and handed her several typewritten pages, held together with a paper clip. "I found the sermon preached at your father's funeral. Rev. Harlow Mills was a fine pastor who preached a good sermon." Grace peeked at the front page to see just the sermon title and text: "Greater Love Hath No Man, John 15:13". She folded the pages and put them in her bag, resolving to read them when she was at home by herself, unafraid to shed the tears she was sure were coming.

The drive from Benzonia to Frankfort was short, and so Grace was surprised when Allen pulled off the road. He cleared his throat. "Ahem - before we get to my folks' house, I need to tell you something." Grace braced herself. "It's about my name - it's not Allen. Well, in a way it is, because I only changed one letter."

"What are you talking about?"

He sighed. "My full name is Alden Bradford Hopkins. My mother is bound and determined to prove that I'm descended from John Alden, William Bradford and Stephen Hopkins." At Grace's blank face he added, "The Mayflower? 1620?" Then realization dawned. "Oh, right - you were raised by Germans, and might not have had the full onslaught of American history in school." She laughed, admitting that was true, and that history wasn't her best subject.

Allen explained, "My mother has strong opinions and doesn't hesitate to speak her mind." Suddenly he began laughing. Grace looked at him with some annoyance. "What on earth is so funny?" He replied, wheezing, "Your name! Your new surname, I mean. One of the Mayflower passengers was named Richard Warren. Wouldn't it be the cat's meow if you were the Mayflower descendant instead of me?" Grace, understanding the irony in that statement, began laughing with him.

Walking into the Hopkins' front parlor, Grace felt immediately at home. Allen's mother was tall and slender, with graying hair in a neat chignon and sharp eyes behind wire-rimmed glasses. She peppered Grace with questions about her life in Detroit, how she was adjusting to living in Beulah, and her progress in finding out more about her family. Allen laughed. "Mother, let Grace sit down and relax for a while!" Margaret relented, "I'm so sorry – I always let my enthusiasm for family history get the better of me!"

Dinner was delicious. Margaret and her hired cook served almond crusted trout, head of lettuce salad with Thousand Island dressing, rolls, and fresh strawberries for dessert. At the sight of the Parker House rolls, Grace couldn't help herself and started giggling. Seeing her hosts startled faces she explained, grinning, "The boy next door has a dog he named Parker House – because she's light and fluffy!" Then everyone enjoyed a good laugh.

Conversation came back around to family history, when Allen mentioned that Grace had just gotten her mother's death certificate in the mail. At his mother's encouraging nod, Grace volunteered that her mother had died, not when Grace was an infant, but when she was eighteen months old. "Also," she told them, "I discovered the names of her parents – Marsh Roberts and his wife Eleanor. My middle name is Eleanor," she added. Margaret smiled. "How lovely – you were named for someone!"

After dinner, Margaret served coffee in the parlor and the conversation continued. Margaret talked about her volunteer work with the League of Women Voters and John contributed stories about his years as a ship builder, which included time spent working at the Naval Shipyard in Philadelphia. During a lull, Margaret said, "John, Allen says Grace hasn't heard the story of how Crystal Lake was lowered. Why don't you tell her?" To Grace she added, "John's father was part of the work crew and has told us about it many times."

John Hopkins took off his glasses and polished them, looking pleased to have a new audience. "Well, when this part of the county was settled back in 1860, Crystal Lake wasn't much to look at. Oh, the lake itself was pretty, but there was no shoreline; the trees went right down to the water. A man couldn't even go fishing. The water was much higher than it is now; if you can imagine the floor of the Northway Hotel covered in six feet of water, that'll give you an idea."

"Along about 1872 a man by the name of Archibald Jones came here from Illinois and saw how close Crystal Lake was to Lake Michigan. He declared that a channel should be dug between the two so that small steam ships could make their way into Crystal Lake to harvest the ample supply of timber.[9] He got up a company called the Betsie River Improvement Company and sold shares to finance the shindig. They planned to buy land around Crystal Lake, straighten the existing outlet to the Betsie River, and build a steamboat for this waterway.

He hired a bunch of local boys, including my father and William Case, and they started digging." Here John paused. "There was just one slight problem, though – no one had done an official survey to see if the lakes were at the same level." He coughed and said, "They weren't. Turns out that Crystal Lake was almost forty feet higher than Lake Michigan." Grace's eyes widened as her mind raced ahead of John's story to imagine the outcome.

"When the last pile of dirt was moved and the channel was clear, there was no holding the lake back. Folks said they could hear the roar of the waves in Benzonia, five miles away. And within a month's time, when all the dirt and mud had settled, here we had a nice sandy beach all around the lake. Within a few years the Ann Arbor railroad put in stations at Benzonia and Beulah, and the city folk started coming to spend their summers."

---

[9] Archibald Jones (1811-1890) was born in New York and worked on the Erie Canal as a young man. He formed the Benzie County River Improvement Co. in 1873, resulting in the lowering of Crystal Lake.

"Senator Case is fond of calling it the tragedy of Crystal Lake, but I think it's the best thing that ever happened to this county!"[10] Grace had to agree, trying (and failing) to imagine her little cottage without the green lawn sloping down to the lake.

As Grace and Allen were getting ready to go, Grace drew Margaret aside for a private word. "Tell me – in all your genealogy research, have you ever discovered something bad? Something you wish you didn't know?" Margaret bit her lip and nodded, the sad look in her eyes telling Grace not to press for details. She put her arm around Grace. "I know some of your discoveries are hard to take. I will tell you, though, that if you don't press on you will always wonder."

The day was getting late so Allen and Grace said their goodbyes, promising to return soon. On the way back to Beulah they talked about the suggestions Allen's mother had made, building on Gilbert Doane's list. "We need to visit the newspaper office in Benzonia, to look for your mother's obituary. And the Benzonia cemetery, to see if any of your mother's folks are buried there. Oh, and I agree with Mother that it's high time we take a trip to see the Point Betsie lighthouse, just for fun."

---

[10] William L. Case (1856-1933) was a Michigan state senator and prominent member of the community. His work *The Tragedy of Crystal Lake* was first printed in the *Benzie Record* in 1922 and late reprinted by the Benzie County Historical Society.

# Chapter 22: Point Betsie

It was now the first week of July, and Grace puttered around her cottage, remembering the Independence Day celebrations a few days earlier. Allen had picked her up early in the morning, sporting new red, white and blue suspenders. Together they had cheered the Honor band in their new uniforms, watched races and contests (including a greased pig contest, which Grace had never seen before), had fun square dancing, and listened to an inspirational address given by Dr. Eben Mumford of the Michigan Agricultural College.[11] Remembering what it was like in Detroit a year ago, she thought of the headlines in the *Detroit Free Press*, announcing all the deaths, fires and accidents caused by traffic and homemade fireworks. What a contrast to rural life!

That morning she'd gotten up early, not wanting to waste a second of this beautiful day. Ben appeared soon afterward to pump a bucket of water from the well before heading out to pick cherries on the Kraker farm. "Mother says to let her know when you're out of honey and she'll send you some more." Grace had seen Hannah's beehives not long ago and was amazed at the bees' industry.

The day before she'd gathered her laundry and relished having a laundry tub with an agitator, rather than getting elbow deep in sudsy water trying to get clothes clean. Once they were rinsed and put through the wringer, she hung them on the line outside. Later today Grace would bring in the dry clothes and heat a couple of irons on the stove to starch and iron her aprons.

---

[11] Dr. Eben Mumford (1871-1942) was a professor of Sociology at Michigan Agricultural College, and did give the Independence Day address in Beulah in 1923.

After Ben had gone on his way, Grace heated the kettle on the stove, to get hot water for washing the dishes. After that was done, she planned to wash her hair there at the sink, same as she'd always done in Detroit. Hannah had told her that in warm weather she could wash her hair at the pump outside, but that was a little too primitive for Grace.

At 9 am Grace sat down at her desk, determined to put in the two hours she allotted herself to education every day. Stacked on one side were Wentworth's *Complete Arithmetic*, a Latin grammar, Buel's *Library of American History*, and McGuffey's Sixth Reader. That last one she saved for reading in the evening, as a reward for work well done. It contained gems by Charles Dickens ("Death of Little Nell"), Thomas Gray ("Elegy in a Country Churchyard"), Samuel Johnson, William Cullen Bryant, and others. Grace felt that she was finally beginning to catch up with her peers.

In fact, in just the couple of months that she had been here, she had discovered a deep love for English literature. She was soaking up, like a sponge, the timeless words of Tennyson, Shakespeare, Wordsworth, Milton, Coleridge, and many others. A seed was germinating, and Grace was beginning to wonder if she might dare to follow in her benefactor's footsteps and become a teacher.

There was no denying that distractions abounded here. If it wasn't Hannah whisking her off to a shopping trip in Traverse City ("you need to get a bathing costume if you're going to live on a lake!") or Ben begging her to come hunt morel mushrooms or pick berries with him, then it was Allen dropping in to see her.

As if to prove her point, Grace heard the familiar sound of Allen's car pulling up outside. Pushing aside jumbled thoughts of Christopher Columbus and Elizabeth Barrett Browning she got up from the desk and went outside to greet him.

He leaned out his open window and asked, "Doing anything today?"

"Just the usual – study and housework. What did you have in mind?"

"Well, I thought today would be a good day to take a trip to see the Point Betsie lighthouse. And while we're out and about we could swing by the *Benzie Banner* office in Benzonia." Grace thought that was a swell idea and said as much. "Just give me a few minutes to change clothes and pack a lunch." Allen called after her, "Bring Parker – she can go for a run on the beach!"

Soon they were heading north on Crystal Drive, Parker hanging out the back window, barking at anything that moved. As they passed the whitewashed stand that was the Cherry Hut, they waved to Dottie Kraker and her helpers. Just as they turned left on the paved surface of M-22 to continue along the shoreline of Crystal Lake, Allen had to stop the car to let a flock of wild turkeys cross the road.

After just a few miles he turned right, back onto a gravel road covered with sand that rose up a slight incline. As they reached the top, Grace saw Lake Michigan spread out before her, with a red and white lighthouse at the end of the road. Leaving lunch in the car for the moment, they got out and began walking the rest of the sandy road toward the beach, Parker racing ahead of them. Allen picked up a stick, threw it far ahead and shouted, "Parker, fetch," and she was off and running.

Allen started telling her about the area, "Point Betsie lighthouse has been here since the late 1850s, and I think it's one of the prettiest lighthouses I've ever seen." They got to the water's edge, and following Allen's example, Grace took off her shoes and set them in a clump of grass.

As they walked slowly in the shallow water, Grace noticed that Allen was paying close attention to the sand as he walked, and she soon found out why. He stooped and picked up a rock and handed it to her with a look of satisfaction. "Here you go – a Petoskey stone for you to take home!" Grace was delighted at the delicate geometric design, looking like a spiderweb, and entranced when Allen explained that it was a type of fossilized coral. He bent again and handed her a couple of brilliantly colored stones. One was orange and the other green, both with white and gray streaks. "These are agates," he explained. 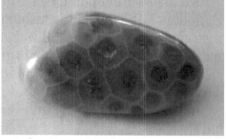 "They're more prevalent up near Lake Superior, but we can still find them here." As he talked, he played with Parker, throwing the stick far down the beach for her to fetch again.

As they walked, Grace had noticed a hustle of activity to the south of them. From a large building several men rolled a long boat down rollers, jumped in once they got to the water, and then paddled furiously for all they were worth. Allen noticed her curiosity and explained, "That's the Coast Guard station, and the men are practicing lifesaving drills. Forty-odd years ago a ship filled with iron ore went down, and the Point Betsie lifeguards saved most of the ship's crew. There's another station further south near Frankfort."

He continued, "If you like, you can consider this your lesson in Michigan history and geography. Over there to the north are the Manitou Islands; the water in between is called the Manitou Passage. Michigan has more lighthouses than any other state, probably because we border four of the Great Lakes. Beyond the Manitou Islands is Beaver Island – now there's a story for you!" Grace looked at him inquiringly. "Until the mid-1850s it was home to 'King James' and his colony of renegade Mormons who broke away from Brigham Young and Joseph Smith."[12]

Grace asked, fascinated, "What happened?"

"James Strang was assassinated, and his followers scattered. The Irish Catholic fishermen who had fled the island ended up coming back and booting out the religious nuts and retaking their land. The island is turning into somewhat of a resort area; a good place to get away from it all!"

Allen whistled for Parker House and together they retraced their steps and retrieved their shoes, and then ate lunch in the car, sheltering from the wind coming off the lake. With a last look at the red and white lighthouse, Allen and Grace headed south on M-22 towards Frankfort, and then turned left on M-115 toward Benzonia.

---

[12] James Strang (1813-1856) was a Michigan state representative and broke away from the Mormon church in 1844, when he established his colony on Beaver Island.

# Chapter 23: Newspapers Again

It wasn't but a few minutes before Allen pulled into a dirt parking lot off the main road in Benzonia, in front of a small office building. "Here we are," he said, "the offices of our local paper, the *Benzie Banner*." When they walked in, Grace was fascinated to see a couple of women sitting at roll-top desks, typing industriously. Pinned to the wall were a large calendar with publication dates marked, a map of Benzie County, a map of Michigan, and a few old posters from the Great War, featuring Uncle Sam and the Statue of Liberty.

Amid the clatter of typing a man came to the front counter. "Hi there, Allen - can I help you?"[13]

"Yes, Mr. Johnson, we're trying to find an obituary that would have been published in..." Allen turned to Grace, "what was the date of your mother's death?" She told the editor, "My mother died in Detroit on December 21, 1902, but she was raised in Benzonia."

Mr. Johnson leaned over the counter and pointed to the window. "See that cinder block building? That's where we moved all our back issues." He shook his head. "It wasn't but four years ago that the Bear Lake newspaper office went up in flames.[14] Wood building, you know. Decades of back issues burned to ashes. We were determined not to let that happen here." He turned to his desk and picked up a set of

---

[13] Andrew Johnson (1888-1985) was editor and publisher of the *Benzie Banner* from 1922 to 1954.
[14] See "Business Section of Bear Lake Fire Swept," *Battle Creek (MI) Enquirer*, 3 October 1919, p.7, col. 2; digital image, *Newspapers.com* (http://www.newspapers.com: accessed 14 January 2024).

keys and tossed them to Allen. "Here – I know you, so you can go on out and take a look. Just make sure to bring the keys back!"

Allen and Grace walked over to the building; Allen unlocked the door and Grace found the dangling chain that turned on the light. Once again, they were confronted with shelves of newspapers that were not nearly as organized as those in S.C. Thompson's office. Because of the disorganization it took them several minutes to find Charlotte Dorsch's obituary.

### Widow of Edward Warren
### Dies in Detroit

*Long time residents here will remember fondly Miss Charlotte Roberts, daughter of the late Dr. Marshall Roberts, who married Edward Warren some years ago. Shortly after Mr. Warren's tragic death their only child, Grace Eleanor was born. Charlotte and her baby moved to Detroit, where she married Mr. Herman Dorsch. Charlotte Warren Dorsch died earlier this week after a short illness, leaving her husband and daughter to mourn her loss. The burial will be in Acacia Park Cemetery, Southfield, MI.*

Grace looked at Allen. "I wonder when my grandfather Marshall Roberts died?"

He suggested, "Based on what we've found, he died between 1897 and 1902. And if he was a prominent member of the community his death would be front page news." Surveying the shelves, Allen said, "You take this side and I'll take that side. It should go quickly if we're only looking at the front page."

Half an hour passed as they went through the stacks of newspapers, stopping now and then to read aloud an interesting headline. Grace found herself organizing the papers by title and date as she searched, to make future searches easier. It was Allen who found the obituary – sure enough, on the front page of the issue for April 1, 1902, was a headline:

## Respected Benzonia Physician Dies

*Area residents were shocked and saddened earlier this week to hear of the sudden death from apoplexy of Dr. Marshall Roberts.*

*After serving in his infantry unit during the Civil War, Marshall Roberts came home determined to become a physician, and attended medical school in Ann Arbor to that end. There he met and married Eleanor Bassett. Upon graduation, the couple traveled by horse-drawn sleigh in the dead of winter to their new home in Benzie County, where a physician was needed. Dr. Roberts is credited with the early use of aspirin and anesthesia and performed the first successful caesarian section in the county.*

*He leaves behind his son Charles Roberts, on his way here from California, his daughter Charlotte, who is up here visiting from Detroit, brothers Frederick (Ludington) and Herbert (Muskegon), sister Mrs. Aaron Phelps (Detroit) and several grandchildren. Dr. Roberts was predeceased by his wife Eleanor, who died several years ago in Florida.*

*Services will be held at the Congregational Church this Saturday, April 5 at 1 p.m. with interment following in Benzonia cemetery.*

Allen spoke first. "Let's take these issues back to the office and I'll borrow one of their typewriters to copy the articles." Speaking kindly to Parker, who sat up and wagged her tail in hopes of leaving, they went back into the office. Mr. Johnson showed Allen to a vacant desk with a typewriter, and in no time, he had typed up the two obituaries. Watching him, Grace resolved to add typing to her list of things to learn.

Although very satisfied that her folder of information was getting fatter every week, Grace still wanted more. With every answer came new questions. Her mother had a brother, Charles – was he still alive? And her aunt and uncles; she would have to track them down. It seemed that she had several cousins, and this was only on her mother's side of the family.

As they were walking back to the car, Grace stopped dead in front of a dusty storefront window and squealed in delight. "Allen, look – a bookstore! Can we go inside, just for a minute?" With a resigned look Parker sat back down on the cement, and Allen followed Grace into the store. She'd never been to a bookstore before, and the thought of all these books being available to purchase was intoxicating. She was drawn to a section of shelves labeled "Local History" and started browsing through the titles there.

By the time they went to the front counter she had a towering stack, with Allen holding a couple as well. There were books on the history of Benzonia Congregational Church, the Benzonia Academy, a 1915 atlas of Benzie County, and an 1884 history of the Grand Traverse region. These reference books would serve to help her become better acquainted with her new home.

Talking about their afternoon as they drove along Crystal Drive, Allen pulled up in front of the cottage and cut the engine. Suddenly he saw the the that the front door was ajar and asked, "Hey, did you leave your front door open?" Startled, Grace replied, "Of course not!" Allen told her, "Stay here a minute while I check things out." In a few minutes he was back and said, "No, don't come in. Take Parker and go to Hannah's house and stay there; I'm going for the sheriff."

When Allen got back with Sheriff Miller following him, Hannah and Grace were waiting just outside the front door. Grace was shivering and fighting back tears, holding Parker in her arms for comfort. The two men went inside and, in a few minutes, when it was obvious the intruder was long gone, they beckoned the women inside.

Grace was appalled at the mess. Dishes were broken and chairs overturned, and most of the books from the shelves behind the desk were lying in a muddled heap on the floor. Grace was grateful that she'd put the crazy quilt away in the cedar chest at the foot of her bed, because the woolen blanket draped over the davenport had been slashed. However, the contents of the desk seemed to be undisturbed.

"Ma'am, can you tell if anything is missing?" Grace shook her head. "Not that I can tell." The sheriff continued, "The point of entry seems to be the back door – it looks like the lock has been picked. Easy enough to do, I suppose, if you know how."

Grace ventured an opinion. "Do you think it might have been those pesky investors trying to frighten me into selling?" Sheriff Miller shook his head. "After that last incident, I escorted them to the depot myself and saw them off on the train to Grand Rapids. No, it wasn't them. This is someone with a personal vendetta."

After Sheriff Miller left, Hannah and Allen pitched in to help Grace clean up. They found that the destruction looked worse than it was; only a few dishes were broken. They picked up chairs and replaced books on the bookshelves; those seemed to be undamaged as well.

Allen proposed that from now on Parker would always remain in the cottage, even when Grace was gone. Privately, Allen doubted if even a barking dog would scare off this determined intruder.

# Chapter 26: An Unexpected Visitor

Berthe Dorsch Shroeder took her valise from the porter and turned to survey the small train depot before her. This Beulah station was nothing like the Central Station in Detroit! Dressed from head to foot in black bombazine, as befitted her advanced years and station in life, she made her way to the ticket counter.

"You, there," she addressed the mustached man, reading what she assumed was the local rag. "Is there such a thing as a hotel in this Godforsaken place?"

He looked up, mildly surprised, but did not let his expression change. "Yes, madam. We have several resorts in the area – Van Deman's, the Cold Brook Inn, the Northway Hotel, the Mollineaux..."

She pounced on the last one, as sounding the most refined. "How do I get to the Mollineaux?"

He leaned over and pointed. "Fred Small's livery stable is right there, just a block away. He'll take you." He added, "That is, *if* the Mollineaux has any rooms available; the resorts are always full to bursting this time of year." He watched as she took her valise and strode away, murmured to himself, "My, my, my," and returned to his newspaper.

The next morning found Grace in her kitchen, having breakfasted and done her daily chores. She was taking a break from her studying to page through her latest women's magazine, deciding on a new recipe to try. The quick breads seemed to be easy enough, and she was trying to choose between Sally Lunn or spoon bread, when there was a sharp rap at the front door. Feeling very thankful for Parker's protective presence, and irritated at the interruption, she rose and crossed the room. Yanking the door open, she started to say, "What....?" Before she could finish her sentence, Grace was enveloped in the ample bosom of her aunt.

"Tante Berthe!" Grace said, once she was free, "What a surprise! Is everything all right at home?"

"I told your dear Papa that I couldn't sleep another night until I came here in person to make sure you weren't withering away in the frozen north. Imagine my disgust when they informed me at the hotel last night that you don't have a telephone, or electricity! What is this world coming to?"

Grace grinned. "No running water, either – I'm managing with a pump and an outhouse. This is really roughing it!" She was thankful that all evidence of the break-in had been cleaned up. If her overbearing aunt had any notion of the escalating attacks, she would whisk Grace back to Detroit at once.

After the two women had eaten lunch and washed dishes, Berthe went to her valise and pulled out a cardboard box and a faded red book. Sitting down at the table again, she motioned to Grace. "Your Papa sent you some things that he has been saving for you. He could just never find the right time...." Grace finished the sentence, "...to spring such a huge surprise on me. It's all right, Tante Berthe, I've come to terms with it now. And he is still my beloved Papa!"

"These are some documents and newspaper articles that he's been saving over the years," Berthe said, handing her the box. Grace opened it and was not surprised to see some of the same items she'd been collecting, as well as some unfamiliar ones. There was her mother's death certificate, and the funeral program. The short obituary from the *Detroit Free Press* she hadn't seen before, but it didn't tell her anything new. The two photos on card stock, of her mother and father, were larger versions of the ones in her locket. New to Grace, though, was the photo of her mother and Papa on what must have been their wedding day. Underneath it was a photo of her mother holding a baby – Grace – on her lap.

"I have this for you, as well," Berthe said, calling her attention back to the present. "Your mother gave it to me for safekeeping just before she died." With that, she handed the book to Grace. *When Knighthood Was in Flower*, Grace knew, was a best seller when it was published in 1898. She opened the cover and on the flyleaf she read,

*To Charlotte*
*From Edward*

*"I bask in the light of many a fair smile."*

Grace blinked back tears. "Oh, *Danke*, Tante Berthe – I will treasure this!" She looked at her aunt. "You knew my mother, didn't you? Tell me, what was she like? Papa never would talk about her."

Berthe thought for a moment. "Yes, I did know your mother from the time she married your Papa until her death. She was as smart as a whip – you take after her. But she had one failing." Berthe sighed again. "I don't know where or when she attended a lecture, but she became enamored of Mary Baker Eddy's theology – Christian Science." She looked at Grace. "I don't know how much you know about them, but their primary belief is that illness and death don't exist. They believe illness and death are illusions." She snorted. "In fact, according to them, you and I are illusions - figments of our own imaginations! So, when she started having some serious pain in her side, instead of calling a doctor she called a Christian Science Practitioner to pray over her." Grace had a revelation and exclaimed, "That's what the C.S.P. on her death certificate stands for!" Berthe nodded. "I'm sure of it. And your poor Papa could not get Lottie to consent to see a doctor until it was too late. It has weighed on him ever since."

Berthe stood up from the table and stretched. "Now, *mein Liebchen*, how about you show me around your little castle?" Grace beamed and took her around the cottage. They went up into the attic, where Berthe made several suggestions for improving the space. Grace had to grin with each sentence that began with "You know what you should do...." She guessed it came from being the oldest sister of a large German family; all Berthe's grown children had learned to say earnestly, "Of course, Mother" and then do just as they pleased.

Outside in the garden was where her aunt proved her worth. Decades of gardening had sunk into her bones, and she was able to identify several mystery plants for Grace. In addition, she suggested flowers for different areas of the yard that would make this cottage a showpiece, as well as vegetables that would grow well here in the north. "A garden should be useful as well as ornamental, that's what I always say!"

# Chapter 26: Letters

Grace had decided it was time to write to Gilbert Doane again, requesting help.

> *Dear Mr. Doane,*
>
> *Since I last wrote I've made some progress in finding out about my family. I found the obituary for my maternal grandfather and am enclosing a copy here. Is there any way of tracking down my uncle Charles Roberts, or my great-uncles Frederick and Herbert Rogers and my great-aunt Mrs. Aaron Phelps? I have several cousins on my mother's side, and I would love to meet some of them.*
>
> *The obituary also mentions that Eleanor Roberts died in Florida "several years ago." However, the Benzonia newspapers from that time have not survived. Can I request a death record from Florida, even if I don't know the exact date or place of her death?*
>
> *A friend's mother is also interested in genealogy and has mentioned census records as another valuable record set. What are these, where are they kept, and how can I access them?*
>
> *Thank you so much for your help!*
> *Grace*

About a week later Grace received a large envelope in the mail. In it were several documents and a response from Mr. Doane.

> *Dear Grace,*
>
> *Last week I happened to be at the state library in Lansing and checked their collection of city directories. It appears that Frederick Roberts died in Muskegon between 1912 and 1913; his widow Eva is still living there. I've attached her address, as well as Herbert Roberts' address in Ludington.*
>
> *Mrs. Aaron Phelps (first name Florence) has moved to Dearborn, and I've included her address as well.*
>
> *The United States began taking a census every ten years in 1790. They did not include every name in each household until 1850. These are kept in bound volumes at the National Archives in Washington D.C., and currently would not be helpful in your search. Just a couple of years ago the 1890 census records were mostly destroyed in a massive fire. Genealogists will be mourning that loss for generations to come.*
>
> *However, there are other records at the National Archives that may be useful. I recommend obtaining Marshall Roberts' Civil War pension and military records. I have attached the names of a couple of researchers in Washington D.C. who would be able to view the records and write a report for you.*
>
> *As for the death record for Eleanor Roberts in Florida, there probably isn't one. Florida*

*began keeping track of vital records less than
ten years ago. Your best option is to locate your
Roberts aunt and uncles and interview them to
try to narrow the time frame of Eleanor's death.
With that you can look to hire a local researcher,
or even take a trip to Florida yourself.*

*Hoping this finds you well,
Sincerely,
Gilbert Doane*

Grace lost no time in writing letters to her great uncle Herbert
Roberts and great aunt Florence Phelps, using much the same format
for each one.

*Dear Great-Uncle Herbert,*

*I hope this finds you well. I just recently
discovered that my mother, Charlotte Roberts
(Warren) Dorsch was the daughter of Marshall and
Eleanor Roberts, and that she grew up in Benzonia.
She died in Detroit when I was very young, and I
was raised by my stepfather.*

*I am eager to know more about my family,
especially Eleanor Roberts, of whom I know very
little. My grandfather Marshall Roberts' obituary
mentioned that she died in Florida many years ago
– do you know when and where? Do you have any
photographs of my Roberts grandparents?*

*Thank you so much for any help you can give
me.*

*Sincerely,
Grace Eleanor Warren*

Grace didn't have to wait long to receive responses.

*Dearest Grace,*

*I met you only once, when your dear mama brought you to see me long ago, but I have fond memories of that visit. Please do come see me in Dearborn next time you visit Detroit. I have some things to give to you, including the family Bible. It has names and dates going back to the Revolutionary War.*

*I'm so glad you're living in Benzie County now – it was your grandfather Marshall's favorite part of Michigan, ever since he moved there.*

*Please visit soon. I have lots of stories to tell you.*

*Much love,*
*Great Aunt Florence*

*Dear Grace,*

*How nice to hear from you! Ludington is only a few hours south of Benzonia, so I had the chance to visit my brother Marshall and his growing family many times over the years. I remember Charlotte very well. I was delighted when she was admitted to Benzonia Academy and saddened to learn of her death.*

*As I recollect, Eleanor traveled to Center Hill, Florida about 1885 to care for her sister who had just given birth. She and her sister both took sick and died; I don't remember what happened to Eleanor's infant nephew.*

*I no longer travel because of my advanced age. Please feel free to come and visit any time.*

*Sincerely,*
*Herbert Roberts*

# Chapter 27: The Storm Breaks

It was getting near the end of August, and the last break-in was several weeks ago. Grace and everyone around her hoped that the intruder had gone away for good, but she was still hesitant to give Parker back to Ben. There had been a long stretch without rain and everywhere Grace went the conversation always veered toward the dry weather and danger of fire.

One Saturday night Grace and Parker had dinner over at Hannah's house, and the evening grew late as the two friends visited, sharing stories about their growing up years. To her surprise, Grace learned that Hannah had grown up in the Upper Peninsula, in a little town called Naubinway. She was full of stories of taking the ferry back and forth between Mackinaw City and St. Ignace and collecting agates from the shores of Lake Superior.

Finally, Grace and Parker said their goodbyes and walked back to the cottage. The air had suddenly gotten cooler and there were dark clouds blocking the stars. Could they finally see rain at last? Suddenly Grace noticed that Parker's fur was standing on end, and she was sounding a low growl. "Hey, girl – what is it? Don't you like thunderstorms?"

Once in the cottage, Grace went around closing the windows against the possible threat of rain, and then took Parker to the bedroom. Yawning, she put on her nightgown and crawled into bed. Parker was sitting upright on the bed, fur still ruffled, refusing to lie down, and occasionally emitting a low growl. "Hey – you've seen rain before, probably even a thunderstorm or two. Relax!" Grace was soon asleep, but Parker kept vigil, not relaxing for a moment.

A few hours later Grace was awakened by the sound of Parker barking furiously. In the distance was the distinct rumble of thunder, getting closer every minute. She thought that was what Parker was barking at, but then she smelled the smoke.

Leaping out of bed, she grabbed her satchel with her folder of information, snatched the crazy quilt from the foot of the bed, and then went to the open door of her bedroom. The smell of smoke was stronger now, and Grace saw tendrils of smoke curling around the back door. The porch was on fire!

Grace yanked open the front door of the cottage and stumbled outside, dropping Parker who had not stopped barking. Grace grabbed the bell rope and pulled with all her might, several times. Even though she was prepared for it, the deafening noise of the clanging bell was startling in its loudness, and within seconds she saw the lights come on at Hannah's house, along with other lights further down Crystal Drive.

Soon Hannah and Ben were at her side. Hannah was urging Grace toward her house while Ben ran toward the pump and started pumping water into the waiting bucket. Suddenly there was a loud *CRACK* of thunder and the heavens opened. No need for buckets of water now; the heavens were supplying their own.

Shortly Allen appeared, and while he was making sure that Grace was all right, he spotted a tall dark figure lurking in the bushes. Calling out, "Parker, fetch!" he picked up a stick from the ground and hurled it, hitting the intruder between the shoulders. Between that blow and Parker yapping at their heels, the figure was soon flat on the ground. To everyone's surprise, it was a woman, who began screeching, "Get off me! The cottage is mine!" Just then Sheriff Miller drove up. He made quick work of handcuffing the suspect and putting her in the back of his car.

"It seems we've caught your intruder, ma'am." The sheriff was triumphant and relieved at the successful conclusion of a puzzling case. "I'm going to take her into town for interrogation, and I'll let you know what happens. But I have no doubt that we've caught the person responsible for the vandalism."

By this time the rain had stopped pouring and settled into a steady drizzle, and Grace and her rescuers were soaked. Hannah shepherded them into her kitchen and started heating water for tea. Grace sat at the kitchen table, using one of Hannah's towels to dry her hair. In the interest of decency, she'd also borrowed a robe. Allen and Ben and a couple of neighbors had fetched some heavy canvas from

Hannah's shed and managed to cover the exposed portion of the porch, after making sure the fire was extinguished.

Allen and Ben came in, wiping their feet and gladly accepting towels to dry off. They stopped to lavish praise on Parker House, who was lying on top of Grace's feet, as if to keep her from going anywhere. "Well, from what we could see in the darkness, the damage appears to be minimal. The back porch will have to be torn down and rebuilt, but the main part of the cottage escaped. Grace, you'll be glad to hear that your books are all fine, if smelling faintly of smoke."

# Chapter 28: To the Rescue

Two days later it was early morning and Hannah and Ben were moving quietly in their kitchen to let Grace sleep. Through the window the outline of the cottage could be seen - the porch shrouded in heavy canvas. Although the perpetrator of the recent violence had been apprehended and locked up, an air of melancholy still lingered. The constant drizzle of rain, though badly needed, didn't help.

When Grace appeared, she had dressed and washed her face and looked more rested than she had since the night of the fire. Hannah put a plate of chicken salad with a cherry muffin on the table and invited Grace to sit down and eat. With the first bite, Grace discovered hunger again and was glad to clean her plate.

While she was eating Hannah updated her on the recent news. "We had two neighbors stop by with food and offers to help rebuild the porch. We are all so grateful that's the only part that was damaged!" Ben came over to join the conversation. "Mr. Randall came over after you were in bed last night and said there's more than enough money in the estate to pay for the repairs." Hannah took over again. "Allen is picking you up this afternoon to have dinner at his folks' house in Frankfort. He said something about having a meeting of minds."

It wasn't even noon, however, when Allen pulled up in front of Hannah's house and blew the horn. Grace came out the front door, shrugging on her duster and stopped when she saw him. "You're looking pretty cheerful," she observed morosely.

He grinned at her. "You're alive, the culprit is caught, and the damage is minimal. Who wouldn't be cheerful? Come on, get in. Mother has prepared a special dinner for you. Oh, and Sheriff Miller flagged me down on the way here. All our intruder would tell him is that her name is Lizzie. She seems rather incoherent, so he's taken her up to the hospital in Traverse City."

As Allen pulled up in front of his parents' blue clapboard house in Frankfort, Grace looked up to see the last person she expected, coming out of the front door. "Chloe! Oh, my goodness! Where did you come from? When did you get here? How long can you stay?"

Chloe hugged her back. "I came from Detroit, silly goose, and I got here late last night. And I'm here for as long as you need me!" Allen chimed in, "It was becoming obvious that you weren't going to send for her, so I did," and was rewarded with a hug and kiss from Grace, which had him blushing.

Once again Margaret Hopkins came through with a meal designed to fortify and nourish. Grace was especially happy to see how well Chloe got on with Allen's parents, especially since she would be staying with them until the cottage was habitable again.

After dinner they all moved to the front parlor to continue their lively discussion, which included plans for a bigger and better porch, what a good dog Parker House was, and speculation on the arsonist. Grace looked over and saw a frown of concentration on Chloe's face. "Grace," she interrupted suddenly, "when we were at Mr. Randall's office in Detroit, didn't he say something about a codicil? That no longer applied since he'd found you?" Chloe, Allen, and Grace stared at each other for a moment. Allen broke the silence first. "Grace, did he give you a copy of the will?" At her shaky nod, he continued, "Do you know where it is?"

Grace nodded. "Somewhere in the cottage." Another moment of silence and the three of them leaped to their feet and ran to the front door, just as Margaret was coming in with dessert. "What in the..." she started. She heard Allen's voice calling as he ran across the lawn and leaped over the door of his Packard, "I'll explain later!"

The wild ride from Frankfort to Beulah was one that Grace would remember for the rest of her life. She could tell that Allen was trying to keep to the speed limit, but his foot kept getting heavier on the accelerator. Grace was frantically trying to remember where she'd put the will, and Chloe was not helping one bit, leaning out of her window, and yelling at surprised pedestrians, "Tally Ho! Twenty-three, skidoo!"

When Allen drew up in the cottage's side yard they piled out, ran inside, and came to a stop in the kitchen. Allen started giving directions: "Chloe, you go look in the attic, Grace, check your bedroom and I'll check the bookshelves." But before any of them could move, Hannah and Ben appeared and had to have the situation explained to them. It was Ben who sensibly suggested, "Miss Grace, wouldn't you have put it in the desk?" He blushed when Grace grabbed him, kissed him on the forehead and proclaimed, "Ben, you're an absolute genius!"

Of course, the will was right where Grace had put it, so many months ago, in one of the side drawers. With shaking hands, she flipped to the last page to read the codicil. Her astonishment showed on her face as she heard a loud chorus of voices, "Well, are you going to keep us in suspense?" "What's it say?" "Read it, read it!"

> *"In the event that Grace Dorsch is not found within five years of my decease it is my will that the cottage and all its contents be sold, and the proceeds placed in trust for my sister, Eliza Van Wagoner Perkins Jones..."* Grace looked up and finished the sentence, *"...current whereabouts unknown."*

There was a short silence and all of them shouted together, "LIZZIE!" Sensibly, Allen said, "Grace, let me borrow that typewriter and I'll type up that codicil and take it to Sheriff Miller. He can get it up to the hospital so the doctors can quiz our culprit. But I think we've found our answer as to who it was and why you were targeted."

# Chapter 29: A Revelation

The following day when Allen left work at the courthouse he drove straight to Hannah's house. He and Grace had decided to make a trip to the Case lumber yard there in Beulah, to start getting supplies for restoring the cottage.[15]

While Allen and Leonard Case were tossing around terms like joists and plywood and load bearing walls, another lumberyard clerk came up to Grace. "I hear tell that you're the new owner of The Birches – Grace Warren, is it?" When she nodded, he continued. "Then you'll have met your grandfather Abijah Warren the old ship captain, I'm sure?"

Allen noticed the look of confusion on her face and came over. Grace frowned and said, "Well, we saw his gravestone, down in Manistee?" The clerk shook his head. "Oh, no – that would be your great grandfather, the one whose ship disappeared and was never seen again. That's why there's no dates on the stone. Your grandfather Abijah Warren retired after one too many shipwrecks, as he put it, and bought a big old house up in Empire. His widowed daughter Phoebe keeps house for him."

This was astounding news, that Grace wanted to act upon immediately. She sent a look of appeal to Allen, who shouted to Leonard that he would come back for the materials the next day. He and Grace headed to the car, and the other man shouted after them, "It's at the end of Storm Hill Drive – the one with the widow's walk!"

---

[15] Leonard Case (1900-1978) worked at his father William Case's lumber mill in the early 1920s, and later became a Justice of the Peace.

As they got into the car, Grace asked, "How long does it take to get to Empire?" "About an hour, more or less."

On the drive to Empire, Grace barely noticed the beauty of the trees passing by, with an occasional white-tailed deer grazing on the side of the road. All she could think of was that at last, she was about to meet someone she was related to. Would they be welcoming, or would she be seen as a fraud?

In the old clapboard house on a bluff overlooking Lake Michigan, Phoebe Strickland couldn't seem to settle down. Over by the fireplace, she picked up one seashell after another from the mantelpiece, then put it in a slightly different spot. Drifting over to her chair, she sat down to take up her knitting, then put it down to go look out the window.

"What in tarnation has gotten into you, girl? You're acting like grease on a hot griddle!"

"I don't know, Father," Phoebe fretted. "I just feel uneasy in my mind somehow."

She walked over to the table where the latest *Benzie County Patriot* was laying and picked it up for the fifth time that morning. Her eyes returned to the lines that had first caught her attention: "There's a new resident at The Birches on the North Shore of Crystal Lake, and the talk around town is that she already has a beau!"

"The Birches," Phoebe murmured. "Why on earth does that sound so familiar?"

Abijah Warren put down the miniature ship he was carving and considered the question. "Wait – wasn't that the name of the cottage owned by that professor lady? Miss Van Something?"

Phoebe looked at him. "Yes – Professor Van Wagoner. I wonder..." Looking at the paper again, she said, "I don't suppose...." And looked at her father again, the look of hope in his eyes mirroring her own. He cocked his head, listening. "Is that an auto I hear?"

Grace barely waited for Allen to stop the car before she tumbled out the door and ran up the steps of the old house. She'd had a quick impression of a faded gray frame house, two stories topped with a balcony facing Lake Michigan, the "widow's walk" they'd been told to look for.

She knocked on the door, heart hammering in her chest. When the door opened, she knew it was her Aunt Phoebe, who seemed to recognize her at once. "Oh, Grace, honey – how I have longed for this day!" The two women hugged for several minutes while Allen waited patiently at the bottom of the steps. Finally, Grace remembered her manners. "Aunt Phoebe, this is my friend Allen Hopkins, who has been helping me ever since I moved to Beulah this past spring."

Phoebe motioned to Allen. "Come in, both of you. Grace, come meet your grandfather – he's in the front room. Father, look who's here!"

The next hour was full of conversation, questions, and answers from all sides with nary a lull. At one point Phoebe went into the kitchen and fixed a simple lunch of sandwiches and fruit. Grace held the floor at the beginning, explaining about her life in Detroit with Herman and Maude Dorsch ("that's why we couldn't find you – we were looking for Charlotte Warren!" exclaimed Phoebe). She also talked about the surprising letter from Mr. Randall, and her subsequent move to The Birches on Crystal Lake.

"And on my first morning there, I found a letter from Professor Van Wagoner in the desk, saying that I was born there in Beulah. I consulted with a librarian and genealogist named Gilbert Doane, and on his advice, I went to the courthouse to obtain my birth record." Allen interjected, "That's where we met – I'm the county clerk." Grace continued, "That was the first I knew of my birth father's name being Warren. And it wasn't until we found my parents' marriage record at the church that I knew his first name was Edward."

Allen chimed in, "From there we went to Manistee, where we found Edward and Charlotte's marriage record, as well as Edward's death certificate. We visited an old newspaperman, S.C. Thompson, who helped us find newspaper articles."

Grace said, "And we paid a visit to Oak Grove cemetery, where we found my father's grave. And a grave for Abijah Warren, and naturally I thought..." Her grandfather finished the sentence, "...that he was your grandfather. No, that's the memorial stone for my father. His ship disappeared in the Atlantic Ocean when I was a young man. My mother remarried and we came out here to Michigan and settled in Manistee."

Then Grace, assisted by Allen, launched into the tale of her intruder, and Parker waking her up when the cottage was set on fire.

A sudden thought struck Grace. "If we hadn't gone to the lumberyard for supplies to rebuild, we might never have learned you were still alive!"

As the afternoon transitioned to evening, Phoebe turned to Grace and said imploringly, "Won't you come and stay with us while your cottage is being rebuilt? We have so many years to catch up on!" Grace agreed immediately and Allen suggested, "Hannah is going to be wondering what happened to us! Why don't I take you home to Beulah and she can bring you back here in the morning. I know she'll want to meet your grandfather and Aunt Phoebe." This seemed like the perfect solution: a chance for Grace to pack a bag and get some rest and for Hannah to meet her family.

It was hard to say goodbye, even if only for a few hours. Phoebe suggested, "Come early tomorrow morning and I'll fix breakfast! Oh, and be sure to bring Parker, too – I want to hug that rescue dog!"

Later that night, when Allen drew up into Hannah's driveway and her door opened, Grace was out of the car and up the walkway in a flash. "Hannah – you'll never guess who we found this afternoon!"

# Chapter 30: Stories From the Past

The following morning as promised, Grace, Hannah and Ben, accompanied by Parker, sporting a new pink ribbon and matching pink leash, drew up to the Warren home in Empire. Grace marveled at the way her life had turned from the near tragedy of the fire to incredible joy in just a few days. She led the way up the front steps and once everyone was inside, made introductions all around.

Phoebe had been busy. The dining room table was set with her best china and silver; there were two lit candles and a bouquet on the table; and coffee and juice were ready to pour. After Grandfather Abijah said a brief, heartfelt blessing, everyone dug into sausages, fried potatoes, waffles, and fresh fruit. Grace scarcely noticed what she was eating; she was so filled with happiness at being with family.

The conversation was lively, filled with laughter and storytelling, and when everyone was done eating, they moved to the front room. After a couple of hours Hannah stood. "I still have chores to do at home, so I'd best be going. Grace, I know Allen will be back here in a couple of days to let you know how the rebuilding is coming along."

Grace got a last hug from Ben, and kissed Parker on her fluffy head, and then waved them off from the front porch. As she came back into the house, Phoebe smiled. "Here, get your bag and I'll show you upstairs to your room." As they climbed the blonde oak stairway Phoebe explained, "Your grandfather sleeps downstairs now; he can't manage the stairs easily any longer."

The guest room at the head of the stairs was a haven of rest. Papered in pale blue wallpaper, there were white dotted Swiss curtains at the window overlooking Lake Michigan. On the four-poster bed was a quilt in shades of blue and green, with seashells around the border. There was a pile of books on the nightstand next to the bed, and Grace caught a glimpse of the titles: *Treasure Island, Kidnapped,* and *At the Back of the North Wind.* Without being told, she knew these books had belonged to her father. Turning to look out the window, she saw that on top of the tall chest of drawers there were three framed photographs of Edward Warren: as a baby, as a young man, and the same wedding portrait she'd already seen.

Phoebe was urging her to come back downstairs, "we'll get some more coffee and sit and visit. We need to tell you about the rest of your family!"

Once they were back in the front room, Grace went to the chair she'd assumed the moment she met Grandfather Abijah – right next to him, so they could hold hands. Aunt Phoebe put another log on the quietly crackling fire, and then went into the kitchen to finish cleaning up after breakfast. Soon she brought out a tray with cups of coffee, cream and sugar, and a plate of dark molasses cookies. This morning Grace had the forethought to sit down equipped with a notepad and pencil: she wanted to record all these memories, names and dates that were new to her.

Grace spoke first, feeling a bit hesitant. "Grandfather, could you tell me about my father? I just found out about him so recently, and all I have is his picture in my locket." With that she fished her locket from around her neck and held it out for Phoebe to look at. Wistfully, Phoebe said, "That's the locket Charlotte wore every day."

Grace asked, "My father's obituary stated that he wanted to study for the ministry; did you know of that?" Abijah Warren snorted and shook his head. "I come from a long line of seafaring folk, and Edward wanted to break out of that mold. Said he didn't want to chance dying by drowning." Phoebe chimed in sadly, "And we all know how that turned out." She brightened a little and looked at Grace. "The little girl he saved, Anna Becker? She grew up, got married and lives in Petoskey now. Just last month she brought her little boy to see us – she named him Edward."

Grandfather Abijah looked stern and said gruffly, "In this family, we have retired the name 'Edward' and will no longer use it. One of our ancestors, Edward Warren, fought with Lafayette in the

Revolutionary War." Phoebe took up the tale she'd heard many times before. "He drowned in the Naugatuck River in 1814."[16]

Over the next hour Abijah Warren held the floor as he told stories of shipwrecks, pirates, and being marooned at sea. "My great-grandfather Absalom Beecher, now – he had to get a seaman's protection certificate during the War of 1812, to prove he was a United States citizen." He snorted. "Not that it did him much good – the British boarded his ship and impressed him into service anyways. But he eventually escaped."

Phoebe urged, "Father, tell about your last shipwreck, the one that made you decide to retire."

Abijah smiled, remembering. "That was the steamer *Marshall Butters*, sailing out of Manistee. She went down in Lake Erie in October 1916, and the first dispatches said that all hands were lost.[17] Imagine everyone's surprise when I turned up on my doorstep alive and well!" Phoebe contributed, "For me, that was the last straw. I told Father he had to retire, or else!"

Grandfather continued. "Farther back, I was on the schooner *Trinidad* when it sank in Lake Michigan just after we sailed through the straits of Mackinac. It was hauling coal and iron, which all disappeared beneath the waves."[18]

Talk turned to naming family members for Grace, and she was kept busy scribbling names and dates: her father's siblings, her grandfather's siblings, and details about her Grandmother Julia Warren who had died long ago. She lost count of the number of cousins she had, and Phoebe promised, "We'll have a family get-together, maybe over Labor Day."

---

[16] See *Find a Grave* (https://www.findagrave.com/memorial/24208894/edward-warren).

[17] The *Marshall Butters* sank in a storm in Lake Erie on 20 October 1916. Everyone aboard survived. See "Fate Unknown," *The Dayton (Ohio) Herald,* 21 October 1916, p.3, col. 3; digital image, *Newspapers.com.*

[18] See "Marine Disasters," *The Watertown (Wisconsin) News*, 18 May 1881, p.2, col. 1; digital image, *Newspapers.com.*

# Chapter 31: Visiting Hours

Several days later Grace was in the kitchen. She finished packing her basket, then looked around to make sure she hadn't forgotten anything. Coming in from the front room, her aunt asked her again, "Are you sure you want to do this?" Grace bit her lip and nodded. "Aunt Phoebe, I need to do this. Don't worry about me – Allen is coming with me, and I'll be quite safe. " She paused. "You know what's been going through my head? 'Blessed are the merciful, for they shall obtain mercy.'" Aunt Phoebe countered good-naturedly with, "Be sober, be vigilant, because your adversary the devil, as a roaring lion, walketh about, seeking whom he may devour." They both laughed and called it a draw. Grace had decided to go back home to Beulah, as the cottage was ready for her.

Outside, a horn sounded. Grace grabbed her coat and basket, gave her aunt a quick hug, and then was out the door and down the steps before she could lose courage. Allen opened the car door for her, not bothering to question her as Aunt Phoebe had done. He had already argued his case against what Grace was doing and had lost. He considered it a minor victory that she had at least allowed him to drive her to Traverse City.

During the hour-long drive, they both were silent, thinking about the confrontation ahead of them. Grace found herself thinking back on all that had happened since her arrival in Beulah, with the episodes of violence getting worse each time, and feeling very thankful that they were no longer a threat.

At the end of their journey, Allen pulled up the car in a visitor space and turned it off. "Here we are," he said, as they both gazed up at the imposing gray stone buildings of the Traverse City State Hospital. He helped Grace out of the car, and taking her hand, they walked together, following the signs to the hospital office. As they walked, Grace commented on the neat appearance of the grounds. "I've read that they employ some of the patients in the gardens and greenhouses."

"Yes, and I've heard that the hospital grows its own flowers, fruits and vegetables, saving a bunch of money. It's probably good therapy for the patients, as well." Allen nodded at a couple of probationers in their blue and white uniforms, accompanied by a more senior nurse with the distinctive black stripe on her cap. Allen remarked, "You know, as recently as ten years ago this place was known as the Michigan Insane Asylum. 'Traverse City State Hospital' sounds a lot better."

Inside, they waited only a few minutes before the doctor in charge of Mrs. Lizzie Jones' care ushered them into his office. Dr. Martin sat down at his desk and opened a file. He looked at Grace. "May I note you as Lizzie Jones' next of kin? She has no children, and as far as we could ascertain, no other extended family." Grace readily assented. He continued to describe his questioning of Mrs. Jones and the somewhat less than satisfactory results. "Our patient is of substandard intelligence, and we suspect that there may have been some brain damage at her birth. In any case, she'll be here for the rest of her life."

He cleared his throat and continued, "It's not many people who would consent to visit their attacker, demented or not." Grace nodded in agreement, as Allen interjected, "I tried to dissuade her, but she can be stubborn at times..." She tried to explain, "I know what she did was wrong, but in a way, I understand it. If I'd been expecting to inherit the cottage and then had it yanked away from me, I don't know what I would have done."

Dr. Martin rose. "We've set aside a small conference room for you; if you'll just follow me." They proceeded a short distance down the hallway and into a room furnished with a table and two chairs. Allen looked at Grace and said, "I'll be right outside the door if you need me." The doctor added that there would be a nurse standing guard as well.

Grace sat down, and soon Lizzie Jones entered. She was smaller than Grace had remembered and seemed defeated. She looked at Grace as if in fear and sat down. Suddenly she grinned and said, "You can have the cottage. I likes it here." Lizzie thought for a moment and expanded on that thought. "They feed me. We had gingerbread and tea yesterday, and I got to work in the greenhouse. And you know what's best of all?" Grace, mute, shook her head. Triumphantly Lizzie said, "They don't make me read. Reading makes my head hurt."

Grace opened her basket and said, "I'm glad you don't have to read, and you get to work with the flowers. Here – I brought some cookies to share with you." As they munched companionably, Lizzie opened up about her childhood and Grace gradually got a fuller picture of her troubled life: how she'd always felt diminished next to her brilliant older sister Edith, and how she escaped from home as soon as she could marry. It did not sound like any of her husbands were exemplary characters, either.

After an hour Grace hugged Lizzie and wished her well and watched her walk down the hallway accompanied by the nurse. Allen asked, "Well, how did it go?" Grace laughed and said, "She told me that one of her husbands taught her how to pick a lock, but she couldn't remember if it was her second or her fourth."

They got in the car, and as Allen started it, he asked, "Where to?" Grace kissed him and said, "Home. Home to Beulah."

# Chapter 32: The Kaleidoscope

The summer was approaching its end, and leaves were already beginning to turn. About a week after her visit to Lizzie in Traverse City, Grace was back where she belonged – sitting at her desk, deciding what to study next. There was still a definite fragrance of wood shavings and fresh paint, and the front porch was now half again as wide as before. She looked around the main room, thinking of how little had changed – and yet, so much had changed. She was not the same person who had awakened in the cottage that first April morning.

She picked up the kaleidoscope that Ben had unearthed from the toybox in the attic. Putting it to her eye, she turned the cardboard tube and watched as the bits of colored glass - reminiscent of the crazy quilt – turned and tumbled to form new geometric designs. "Why – that's it!" she said to herself. "Life is just like a kaleidoscope!"

Hearing the mailman out on Crystal Drive, she went out to see if there were any letters for her. To her surprise, there was another large envelope from Gilbert Doane. Standing there by the mailbox she opened it and read the letter lying on top of a stack of papers.

> *Dear Grace,*
> *Your case has interested me from the beginning, and since genealogists are fascinated with others' families, not just their own, I took the liberty of doing additional research. What I found was most interesting.*
> *I am including a short report with the relevant documents, to offer proof that your mother, Charlotte Roberts Warren Dorsch*

*and Edith Van Wagoner were indeed related.
Their grandmothers were sisters, which
means they were second cousins, and you are
Miss Van Wagoner's second cousin once
removed.*

*There's no way of telling if they knew of
this relationship, but you may rest assured
that you are indeed Miss Van Wagoner's heir
and the rightful owner of the property on
Crystal Lake.*

*Yours sincerely,*
*Gilbert Doane*

Grace couldn't help but start laughing. She said aloud, "The kaleidoscope turns again!"

# Acknowledgements

It takes a village to write a book. I discovered that in writing my previous book, *From Pie Stand to Icon: the 100-year history of the Cherry Hut, Beulah, Michigan*, which was published in 2022. Although I did the majority of the research and writing, I also had input from many current and former staff members and conducted interviews by email, phone and Zoom. My experience working with Mission Point Press was terrific as well. In a very real sense, that book was the precursor to *Home to Beulah*.

I must give credit to the Writer's Retreat hosted by Anne Lamott in September 2023. During her keynote speech, she gave us a prompt: "There was a tree." My response to that prompt can be found in Chapter 8: The First Morning. This helped gather all the ideas that had been tumbling in my head for the past two years.

I owe heartfelt thanks to my beta readers: Rahn Carlson Huber, Don DeFerbrache, Luci Fenton, Laurie Stevens, Jane Irish Nelson, Lucy Mahaffey, Kathi Williams, and Mary Kay Elfman. Every one of them found something different to comment on!

My most valuable beta readers are long-time residents of Benzie County. Reverend Ned Edwards was a staffer at the Cherry Hut in the 1950s and later became the founding minister of St. Andrew's Presbyterian Church in Beulah. Larry White is the current president of the Benzie Area Historical Society. Consulting with them was crucial in making this story as historically accurate as possible. (That's why the cottage has no electricity or running water!)

I found the perfect editor in Patricia Desmond Biallas. A genealogist who grew up in Michigan and worked as a professional editor and proofreader, she was the perfect pair of eyes to help make this book the best it could be.

# About the Characters

Although this is a fictional story with made-up characters, I couldn't leave out all the real-life people who were living in Northern Michigan during this time period. Many of them were my ancestors, others I got to know from decades of research. Here is a guide:

**Fictional Characters:**
Charlotte Eleanor (Roberts) Warren
Edward A. Warren
Edith Van Wagoner
Grace Eleanor Dorsch
Chloe McGrath
Mr. Thomas Randall
Hannah Thorpe and her son Ben Thorpe
Alden "Allen" Bradford Hopkins
John and Margaret Hopkins
Capt. Abijah Warren
Phoebe (Warren) Strickland

**Real People:**
Clarence M. Burton (1853-1932) was a Detroit lawyer and philanthropist. The Burton Collection of local history at the Detroit Public Library is named for him.

Leonard Case (1900-1978) was the son of William Case and the grandson of Lucius Case, who came to Benzie County from Ohio in the early 1860s. Leonard worked in his father's lumber mill as a young man and later became a justice of the peace. His grandson Andy Case is the owner and manager of The Cherry Hut in Beulah.

William L. Case (1856-1933) was a young man on the work crew hoping to open a channel from Crystal Lake to Lake Michigan, and recorded his reminiscences in *The Tragedy of Crystal Lake*.

Gilbert H. Doane (1897-1980) was born in Vermont and obtained his library degree at Columbia University in 1921. He worked as Assistant Librarian at the University of Michigan from

1922 to 1925 and Director of Libraries at the University of Nebraska from 1925 to 1937. He was ordained as an Episcopal priest in 1956 and served at Grace Episcopal Church, Madison, Wisconsin. He published *Searching for Your Ancestors* in 1937.

Rev. Ira Fales (1883-1965) was the pastor of Benzonia Congregational Church from 1921 to 1927.

Andrew Johnson (1888-1985) was editor and publisher of the *Benzie Banner* from 1922 to 1954.

Archibald Jones (1811-1890) was born in New York and worked on the Erie Canal as a young man. He formed the Benzie County River Improvement Co. in 1873, resulting in the lowering of Crystal Lake.

James Kraker (1889-1960) and his wife Dorothy Rogers Kraker (1888-1958) were the original owners of the roadside pie stand they set up on Crystal Drive in 1922. It became known as The Cherry Hut and evolved into a renowned restaurant. They bought the land with established cherry orchards on the north shore of Crystal Lake in 1921 – from my great-grandfather, Percy A. Reed.

Rev. Harlow S. Mills (1846-1931) was the pastor of Benzonia Congregational Church from 1896 to 1916. He was instrumental in setting up smaller churches around the county, which he recounted in his 1914 book, *The Making of a Country Parish*.

Dr. Eben Mumford (1871-1942) was a professor of Sociology at Michigan Agricultural College and did give the Independence Day address in Beulah in 1923.

Percy A. Reed (1864-1955) was born in Kalamazoo and married Mary Adeline Beem in Newaygo County, Michigan in 1887. Their oldest son was my grandfather, Maurice L. Reed, born in 1891. Percy and Mary Reed settled in Beulah by 1910, where he owned and operated a shoe store.

Fred Small (1868-1959) was born in Beulah, the son of Shadrach and Angeline (Hill) Small. He became the town veterinarian and owned the livery stable; he also worked on the roads. His youngest son Lewis Arthur Small married my father's older sister, Jane Reed.

James Strang (1813-1856) was a Michigan state representative and broke away from the Mormon church in 1844, when he established his colony on Beaver Island.

Stacy Clay Thompson (1856-1944) was born in Clearfield County, PA and before he reached the age of fourteen walked to northern Michigan with his father and older brothers. He settled in Manistee by 1879, where he ran a newspaper, became a delegate to the Michigan House of Representatives, patented a clothes drying rack and sold real estate. He, his first wife Ida May and most of his family are buried in Oak Grove Cemetery in Manistee.

Edward Warren (1764-1814) was a Revolutionary War soldier who fought at the battle of Ticonderoga and under the command of Lafayette.

# Resource List

"An Architect's Ideal Home," Henry Wright. *Good Housekeeping,* June 1921, p.64; PDF download, *Internet Archive.*

"Armstrong's Linoleum Rugs," *Ladies Home Journal,* January 1921, p.74; PDF download, *Internet Archive.*

Bak, Richard. Detroit, 1900-1930. Images of America. (Charleston, SC: Arcadia Publishing, 1999).

"Beulah – On Picturesque Crystal Lake," *Traverse City (MI) Record-Eagle,* 28 June 1930, p.14; digital image, *Newspapers.com* (http://www.newspapers.com).

Case, William. The Tragedy of Crystal Lake with Some Sidelights. (Benzonia, MI: Benzie County Historical Society, 1978).

Catton, Bruce. Waiting for the morning train: an American boyhood. (Detroit: Wayne State University Press, 1987).

Daniels, Stacy Leroy. The comedy of Crystal Lake: the lowering of Crystal Lake and the biography of Archibald Jones. (Frankfort, MI: Flushed with Pride Press, 2015).

Doane, Gilbert H. Searching for your ancestors: the how and why of genealogy. (Minneapolis: University of Minnesota Press, 1960).

Gaffney, T. J. and Dean Pyers. Pere Marquette 1225. (Charleston, SC: Arcadia Publishing, 2014).

Good Housekeeping's Book of Menus, Recipes and Household Discoveries. (New York: Good Housekeeping, 1925).

Kavanaugh, Kelli B. Detroit's Michigan Central Station. Charleston, SC: Arcadia Publishing, 2001

Lardinois, Anna. Shipwrecks of the Great Lakes: tragedies and legacies from the inland seas. (Guilford, CT: Globe Pequot, 2021).

LeClaire, Virginia M. The Traverse City State Hospital Training School for Nurses. (Traverse City, MI: History Center of Traverse City, 2012).

McGuffey's Sixth Eclectic Reader. (Chicago: American Book Co., 1907); PDF download, *Internet Archive.*

Mills, Harlow S. The Making of a Country Parish. (New York: Missionary Education Movement of the U.S. and Canada, 1914); PDF download, *Internet Archive* (http://www.archive.org)

"One Dead, 39 Injured in Fourth of July Accidents," *Detroit (MI) Free Press,* 5 July 1922, p.1; digital image, *Newspapers.com.*

"Quick Hot Breads," Ida Bailey Allen. *Woman's World*, January 1922. PDF download, *Internet Archive* (http://www.archive.org).

Standard Atlas of Benzie County, Michigan. (Chicago: Geo. A. Ogle & Co., 1915).

Steele, Earle and Kristen Hains. Beauty is Therapy: a memoir of the Traverse City State Hospital. (Traverse City, MI: Denali and Co., 2001).

Tasker, Greg. Sanders Confectionery. Images of America. (Charleston, SC: Arcadia Publishing, 2006).

Yock, Dr. Louis. Crystal Lake. Images of America. (Charleston, SC: Arcadia Publishing, 2009).

Yock, Dr. Louis, Lost Benzie County. (Charleston, SC: Arcadia Publishing, 2011).

# About the Author

Claudia Breland began researching her family in 1974, after she received family papers from her paternal grandfather. She became a professional genealogist in 2009 and has had clients from around the world, and has lectured in Western Washington, Canada and at the National Genealogical Society conference.

She is an avid user of DNA and has solved over 25 cases of unknown parent or grandparent puzzles. Claudia broke a 45-year brick wall, using DNA genetic networks, finding a black sheep 2nd great grandfather who deserted during the Civil War, and discovering a motive for murder in the death of her 2nd great-grandmother in 1883.

*Home to Beulah* is her seventh book and her first novel.

Made in United States
Troutdale, OR
02/16/2024

17748943R00076